CHAPTER ONE

Sean

"Took your ass long enough to get here Bro! I was almost talked into leaving with that cute snow bunny over there," Eli said, double slapping my hand, before nodding at the cute blonde haired chick at the table on the other side of the bar.

"We don't all make our own hours like you man. I had a patient, and ol girl ain't your type no way. Her skin ain't dark enough, and her curves don't look nearly as "Jessica Rabbit" as you like them." I said, nudging my buddy with my elbow.

Eli is my best friend, more like the brother I never had. We met in college and have been tight ever since. Eli had this certain charm about him that always had the ladies wanting to line up and be on his team. It could be the way he looks: tall, samoan, tan and handsome. (I can say that without losing man points right?).

It could also be his personality; after all, that is what drew me in as a friend all those years ago. He has to be, hands down, the most outgoing, fun person I know. He and I meet every monday for happy hour over in the Marina. Eli owns his own trucking company, so he can come and go as he pleases. I work at Kaiser as a pediatric therapist. I don't leave for the day until I'm done.

Eli looked at me with one eyebrow raised, "You're right bro, I'd have to be falling on hard times to start messing around with a bean pole snow bunny." We both laughed.

"Aye Jessica," I said calling to the bartender," can you bring me a beer, and one for this rock head too," I said motioning to my buddy.

"It's one fine ass head too ain't it Jess?" Eli said, smoothing his hands over his long, wavy braided mane.

"When you gon cut those ponytails off man?" I asked, tugging at one of his braids.

"Never! I think the hair is what gives me the power over the coochie. You know I've never had a haircut in my life bro. No need to rock this boat."

Eli was, well, a hoe and proud of it. He had so many woman I always wondered how he kept up with them all. He constantly clowned me for not pulling chicks like he knew I could.

"You're a good looking dude, you know you could have any woman you wanted," he told me at least once a week. I wasn't an "any girl" type of guy though, I knew which one I wanted, and I couldn't wait to go see her.

"You know I gotta get going soon." I reminded him.

"Yea, you gotta go be a creeper at the market. Don't remind me." Eli said laughing.

"I'm gonna talk to her today. I've already pumped myself up for it. She's so BADDD, with some extra D's at the end! I just hadn't worked up the nerve until now." I confessed.

Eli looked at me with a sly smirk creeping across his face. "If you don't holla at her today, you gotta let me hook you up with someone, my choice."

"Hell no! I'm not letting that happen. It's on today." I said getting up. I double slapped his hand before I headed out the door.

"Don't pussy out!"He yelled.

I shook my head at him, and was on my way.

Andrea

"I broke a nail!" Ashlynn said in a whiny voice.

"Girl get over it. You're supposed to be hanging up those dresses we just got in. I don't pay you to play with your nails."

Ashlynn pursed her lips together, rolling her eyes the way she always did when she wanted me to get off her case.

My baby sister is 21 and she's been a slacker her entire life. I'm sure it's because she's the baby of the family. Mom and dad gave her everything her little spoiled heart desired. I'm the oldest, my brother Andrew came 4 years after me.

"Damn Drea, why did you have to order so many dresses? I'll be hanging these up forever! I got shit to do today!" Ashlynn said, flipping her massive reddish-brown ponytail full of curls off her shoulder, her heart shaped caramel complected face showing lines of frustration across her forehead.

"Girl hush, and fix your face. Just do your job! You can handle your business after work. It's almost time to go anyway, so stop complaining and finish up!"

Ashlynn sighed, rolling her eyes. I ignored her, like usual.

Once closing time came, Ash and I balanced the register, and tidied up the store.

"See you tomorrow baby sis. Get here on time, and leave the complaining in the parking lot." I said, hugging her.

Ashlynn sucked her teeth. "See you tomorrow Drea."

She works my nerves, but I would do anything for her, and she knows it.

After work every evening, I drive across the street to Ralph's grocery store to pick up something quick to cook. I'm there so much they know me by name. I grabbed a basket, and headed over to the produce section. I've been trying to eat healthier. My hips are getting a little out of control, and I need to keep that in check. I get these hips from moms side and I'm not trying to get like my aunt June. Her hips are so wide she's always accidentally knocking things over.

I put some fresh spinach and a few sweet potatoes in my cart, now I just needed some protein. Heading toward the meat section, I heard a voice behind me.

"Excuse me."

I looked up to find a tall, chocolate cutie standing next to me.

"Damn he's fine!" I thought to myself. I scooted over thinking I was in his way.

"Excuse me," he said again.

I looked up at him this time, and noticed he was smiling at me.

"I'm sorry, am I still in your way?" I asked.

"Uh no, you're not in my way. I just wanted to introduce myself. My name is Sean, and I see you here all the time.'

"Ok. Hi Sean." I said, smiling. I was caught off guard, I kept a nervous grin on my face. Sean seemed nervous too. He kept fidgeting with his hands and looked down.
He continued.

"Yea, and I think you're really beautiful. I felt like I should come speak to you, get your name, and maybe your...and maybe your number." He said, looking embarrassed.

I smiled at his sincerity.

"My name is Andrea, nice to meet you." I said, extending my hand, giggling. His approach was sweet. Much different than the "Aye Boo!" I usually get from the men I seem to attract.

"Nice to formally meet you too Andrea. That's a beautiful name by the way, it suits you."

"Thank you." I blushed, nervously twirling my long sandy brown curls.

Sean had a beautiful smile, with bright white teeth and a perfectly groomed mustache goatee combo. He had to be about 6'1" with the perfect basketball player's physique. I was instantly attracted to him physically, but even more when he spoke. Everything he said sounded sincere, his deep brown almond shaped eyes sparkling with every word.

"I'd love to get your number, get to know you better, possibly take you out sometime." Sean said.

"That sounds like something we could work out." I giggled. I could feel myself blushing like a stupid schoolgirl. I don't know what it was about this man that had me all out of sorts.

"Hand me your phone, I'll put my number in." I said, smiling.

"Here you go beautiful." He said handing it to me.

"We have the same phone." I said, wondering why I felt the need to point that out.

"Look at us, we think alike already." He said, still smiling. He hadn't taken his eyes off of me since he introduced himself.

"Okay, here you go." I handed him his phone." It was nice meeting you Sean. I need to get back to my shopping."

He deliberately grabbed my hand while taking his phone back . I slid my hand from his blushing, my light brown skin turning 12 shades of red.

I turned and started to walk away, shaking my head at myself for acting out of character.

"Tuck your cool back in Andrea," I said to myself.

"Talk to you real soon Andrea" I heard him say.

I turned back and waved. Sean stood there with a silly grin on his face.

"I really hope he calls" I said to myself. Now let me go get this chicken...

Andrea

"He was so handsome! I don't know what came over me. He had me blushing like a schoolgirl. Like I had never met a man before."

"What did he say that had you all giddy?" Ashlynn asked.

"It wasn't what he said, it was. . I don't know. Just something about him. I can tell he's different. Y'all know I've been single for awhile now. Since I broke up with Mark, I have just been enjoying my single life."

"You really haven't been enjoying it that damn much. I don't know who you frontin' for. And besides, you should probably chill a little bit Drea, you know you fall fast and hard, and always for the wrong men," Jamie said, sifting through the racks of new dresses we got in the day before.

Jamie was my best friend. I met her the first day of freshman year in high school at Westchester. We had algebra together. She sat next to me and we bonded over not knowing what the hell we were doing. From then on we had been inseparable. Around campus people would call us Tom and Jerry since I was so much shorter than her. My 5'2" frame had nothing on Jamie's 5'10" chocolate, curvy voluptuousness. Over the years Jamie had become more like family than any friend I ever had. I had been there for all the important events in her life and she had always been there for me.

"I hope you're not right this time J. Something is just different with this guy. It already FEELS different." I said, wrapping my arms around my own body in an embrace.
Ashlynn scrunched up her face and said,"Well those eggs of yours are close to their expiration date, so you better use them before they go bad." Ashlynn giggled.
Jamie and I laughed loudly. Ashlynn is good with the quips. She learned that from me.

"She can have one of my little divas. I been trying to pawn them off on her for years now."Jamie said referring to her two daughters Giselle and Bella who were five and three and the sweetest little munchkins I knew.
I waved a hand to quiet the peanut gallery down."I'm only 30. I still have some time left. But you're right Ash, I don't want to be trying to make babies with powdered eggs. And I would take one of yours J, but you know you'd want either of them back, while you playin'." I said.

I hadn't thought about having children since I broke up with my ex-boyfriend Mark. I was so in love with Mark I couldn't see straight. We met at a business conference back in 2010. He was smart and good looking. He was tall and for a shorty like me that's always a good thing. He had smokey grey eyes, a chiseled jawline and the perfect almond complexion. What attracted me more than his broad shoulders and his football player build, was his sweet southern accent. He was from Texas and very charming to me. I'd been used to meeting men from my neck of the woods, running into men from other places was rare. I was up for a new challenge.

Mark and I dated for a year and things we going well. My family and friends loved him, aside from Jamie. She told me she got weird vibes from him. I ignored her warnings; I thought the world of him. There was just one thing, in that entire year I had never met any of his friends or family. Any time I would ask, he would have some sort of excuse. That bothered me a lot, but it didn't stop the way I felt about him.Jamie thought that was too strange and told me to press him about it. After all my griping, he told me he would take me to meet his parents. He was going out to Texas for a visit and would send for me. Well he left for Austin and when it was time for me to come, he told me there was a change of plans. He said he didn't have the money for a ticket for me and that he was sorry. He said he would be back in a week or so and he told me he loved me. I was hurt. I came up with the brilliant Idea that I would buy my own ticket and fly out there. I knew where he said his parents lived and I thought it would be a nice surprise. I got to Austin on a friday afternoon and drove myself to his parents house. I rang the doorbell, Mark was shocked to see me. I had never seen a brown brotha turn so pale. He stepped outside and closed the door behind him.

      "What you doing here sweetie?" Mark said.

      "I came to surprise you!" I said with a smile.

      "Oh. .oh. . uh. . .oh that's nice." He said stuttering, looking behind him at the door he walked out of.

"You don't look happy to see me."

"I am, it's just that. . well. . .I wasn't expecting you and. . ."

The door opened and a sweet looking white woman walked out. She was probably a little younger than me with blond hair, blue eyes and a sweet smile. She was curvy with a small waist; built like a cheerleader. She walked up and stood next to Mark. His expression was priceless, he looked like a deer caught in headlights.

"Hey babe, what's going on out here? Who is this?" She motioned toward me, smiling sweetly.

"Oh. . .uh. . .This is. . This is my friend Andrea." Mark said nervously, rubbing the back of his neck.

"Your friend!?" I snapped. I wouldn't have believed what was going on if I wasn't there to witness it myself.

"Mark honey, what's going on?" She said

"Well it looks like he's lost all his damn words. I'm Andrea," I said, extending a hand for her to shake. She shook my hand reluctant, nervous even." I'm just finding out I'm his friend. I was under the impression that I was his girlfriend." I said, not taking my eyes off of Mark.

"What gave you that impression, if you don't mind me asking?" She said, the corners of her mouth trembled as she tried to hold on to that sweet smile.
I turned my attention to her."Well, it could be the fact that we've been dating for over a year now, we just made lov... he just slept with me last week before he came here." Her mouth fell open.

"So," I said, holding my hand up to let this woman know I was done talking to her for now, looking over at Mark," you spending time with family and friends and making love is something you do with all your FRIENDS Mark?" I said glaring at him trying to find some answers.

His white woman looked at him with the same glare trying to get answers too.

Mark had to confess to the double life he had been living. Every time he went home to visit, he was with her, Amber. When he was in california he was with me. He and Amber had been together for 7 fucking years! They were engaged and she was pregnant.I was devastated.

"Lose my got damn number!" I told him and I left right then but not before punching him in the face, square in the nose. I'm sure I broke it; my hand hurt for days. I went back to the airport and made my way back to Cali. I never heard from Mark again and I've been single every since.

Well maybe not single, but not very attracted to anyone I could bring home to my family. I've dated Rashad the thug with no aspiration, Kevin the "wanna be" rapper who had never even been to a real studio, James, the undercover drug dealer, and Will my "Something New" Who turned out to be a wigga in disguise.

I think my picker was broken after Mark, so I decided to stop with the dating. It had been a year and change since I had been on any date much less sexually pleased by any man. All of my focus was on my business and I had planned to keep it that way. That was before yesterday and meeting Sean.

Sean

Inglewood was shaping up to be one of the best moves I'd ever made. After moving into my apartment I needed to stock my fridge so I headed down to the local Ralphs. I aimlessly surfed the aisles trying to find things I didn't have to cook. I was only a pro at making breakfast. I turned down the frozen food aisle and heard a voice talking to someone, I assumed she was on the phone. I looked up and saw the most beautiful woman I had ever laid eyes on, you know, next to my mama. She was petite, maybe about 5'2", with curves to die for. Sista was shaped just like a coke bottle with full breasts, small waist and hips and a butt I could probably sit a drink on. She had long, curly sandy brown hair that was the perfect accent to her light brown complexion, her almond shaped light brown eyes accented by a few freckles on her cheeks and nose. The woman was beautiful and I was enamored by her.

That was the first time I saw her. I walked past her and she looked up and smiled at me. I wanted to say something then, but I had no words. That smile almost knocked me off my feet. Either she had a great dentist like I had, or she was blessed with perfectly straight white teeth. All I could think to do was smile back and keep walking. I felt like a damn fool. I had missed my opportunity.

After that, I would see her at Ralphs every time I went. I started to take note of the times she would come so I wouldn't miss her. Eli called me a creeper when I told him what I had been doing. I didn't need his opinion, I already felt like a creep for just watching her. I know the people in the store probably thought I had a problem. Every time I went I bought a jug of juice and some toilet paper -- random I know -- but I couldn't walk out empty handed. I figured I'd always be thirsty and asses always need wiping. Seeing Andrea had become the highlight of my days. That was 4 months ago, and yesterday I was finally brave enough to make my move. Our brief exchange in the store had me feeling euphoric. Her voice and that smile, made me feel like I was in heaven. Everything she said sounded so sexy floating from her mouth into my headspace. I kept shifting my position and looking at the ground. It was all I could do not to stare at her lips when she spoke. I hadn't planned what I was going to say to her. It shocked me when I heard myself ask for her number. I was even more shocked when she agreed and put her number in my phone.

Now I'm sitting here with my phone in my hand wondering if I should call now. Would that be too soon? Would she think I was too eager? Would playing it too cool be a bad move? Too many thoughts swirling but, I don't want to mess this up, that's what I know for sure. I'm gonna go for it, just not now, "Later" I told myself. I'll call her, but first I need a pep talk. Eli would go into full mack mode if I asked for his advice, so he was out. I think maybe I should run this by Shelby.

"Hey cuzzo! What's up!" Shelby said.

"Hey cuz, not much. What are you up to?" I said, trying to sound collected.

"Not much myself just giving Justin his bath. His bad tail threw his spaghetti all over the place. I probably need to give myself a bath too. Raising a one year old is no easy task,```"she said.

Shelby is my first cousin. We grew up like brother and sister, and she was without a doubt my best friend and I was hers. Growing up if I ever needed to talk about anything she was always there for me and she still is to this day.

Shelby is 32 and married to Lamont. He's a freelance contractor. Right now business is booming for him which affords Shelby the luxury to stay home with their now one year old son Justin. I'm his Godfather and I love that kid to pieces.

Shelby has been trying to hook me up with her friends for years now. I never take her up on the offer because all her friends seem to be ratchet, and I don't do ratchet women. I've been single for at least a year now, but I've never really had a serious relationship. After a few weeks of dating a woman and maybe being intimate with her, I'd find out they were only dating me because they thought I was a come up: a black, handsome (if I do say so myself) successful man. They always thought they had hit the gravy train with me.

My last sorta relationship was with Briana. I met her in the lobby of the hospital. She was there for a checkup and I was on my way to my office. I bumped into her by accident and almost knocked her over. I caught her before she fell. She looked up and me and smiled with the most beautiful eyes. We chatted briefly and to my surprise she asked for my number. I had never met a woman so bold. It was attractive but, that should have been a red flag for me. As pretty as Briana was with her short wavy dark brown hair, cocoa complexion and body out of this world, she had nothing going for her. She didn't have her own place. She had no car and she was always asking me for money. We had only been seeing each other a two months, and she was already asking me to pay her cell phone bill. I think she saw a meal ticket in me like the ones before her and pounced. I'm really glad I never slept with that girl, not that she didn't try. I probably wouldn't have been able to get rid of her if I had. I think I don't know how to choose them.

There has only been one girl I liked a lot back in high school but, she gave me no play.

Shelby said, "You never call me when the sun goes down, everything ok?"

"It's only 7pm Shel, you're acting like it's midnight."

"Oh, my days all seem the same. I thought it was much later." Shelby said with a sigh.

"Being a stay at home mom starting to stress you out?" I asked.

"I'm just starting to feel like I don't have a life anymore. None of my friends have kids so we don't get to hang like we used to. I just need a vacation; a break." She said with another heavy sigh.

"I'll come get Justin this weekend. I haven't had him with me in a while, we could use some bonding time. You know he likes me better than you anyway." I joked.

That made Shelby cheer up a little. I smiled hearing her voice perk up.

"That'll be great Cuzzo. I can get some ME time for a change." She smiled.

"Okay, it's a date with me and my boy then!" I smiled back.

"So what else is on your mind Sean? I know it's something," she said.

"Well... There is something I called to get your advice on," I said, suddenly unsure If I wanted to tell her about Andrea.

"Okay, what's up?"

"Well I met this young lady yesterday and. . ."

"Young lady? How old are you again? She laughed.

"Anyway punk, I met this young lady yesterday. She's beautiful. I got her number and I want to call her but I. . . I'm nervous as hell! I really don't know what to say to her and I don't wanna mess this up," I admitted.

"Cuzzo, why are you trippin'? You act like you've never macked a honey dip before!" She said.

"Macked. . . a honey dip? What year are we in again?" I laughed.

"Shut up jerk, I'm serious. I don't understand why you're nervous. And I hope you called me before you called Eli. He is a damn mess," she said, laughing out loud.

"Leave my boy alone. He can't help it that he's half dog, " panting like a thirsty mutt,"but seriously, I don't know Shel, something about this one. She's not like any other woman I have ever met. I can tell she's different and I just don't want to come off like some lame ass," I said with a sigh.

"Just be you cuzzo. That's all you have to do. Any woman in her right mind would want to be with you, so stop trippin','" she said.

"Okay cuz, thanks for the pep talk. I needed that."

"Anything for you Sean Michael Williams."

"Back atcha Shelby LaQinta Miller." I said with a laugh.

"You know I hate my damn middle name. I told you never say it out loud!"

"LaQunita chill!" I said laughing harder.

"Ugh, I can't stand you! Love you. Bye!"

"Love you too!" I said with a smile.

"I guess there's nothing to it, but to do it." I said aloud as I searched Andrea's number in my phone.

Before I could dial her number there was a knock at my door. I looked at the cable box in the living room and noticed it was 7:35. Who the hell could be at my door this late? No one ever just stops by. I peeped through the blinds to see Eli, I opened the door with a smile.

"Hurry up and let me in Bro! Did you do it!?" Eli asked, stepping inside my apartment.

"What you doing here dude?" I asked, double slapping hands with him the way we did every time we saw each other.

"I was down the street visiting that Big Booty Brandy, and by visiting I mean gettin it in! But whatever, don't change the subject, did you do it!?" Eli said, with a sly smile.

"You always gettin it in with somebody." I said shaking my head.

"And you not ever gettin' it in with nobody. You the most non pussy getting nigga I know, and it ain't like you can't. You done got all religious on me? You a born again virgin?" Eli joked, sitting down on my loveseat.

"You know it ain't nothin' like that. Stop trying to clown me punk. I'm just picky about who I sleep with. You remember how things went with Briana, even you were glad I didn't tap that! But yep, I did it! got her number and everything!" I said proudly, holding up my phone.

"Forreal!? I don't know if I believe you." Eli smiled, making his tight eyes even tighter.

"For real, I did. I'm gonna call her as soon as you get your ass out of here," I told him, slapping his feet off my coffee table.

"What's her name? How you described her I bet it something prissy."

"Andrea." I said with a smile. I liked saying her name.

"Well let me go so you can get your mojo back Bro. I gotta go see Evette now over in Downy." He said walking to the door. He turned around and said," Call me when you get up in that."

I laughed, pushing him out my door. "Alright Dude, I'll holla at you soon," I said double slapping his hand again before I closed the door.

Now where was I? Oh yea, calling Andrea. . .

CHAPTER TWO

Sean

310-452...It's ringing. . .

"Hello" a sweet voice answered

"Uh. . Hello. . . May I speak with Andrea please?" I said hesitantly.

"This is she, and who am I speaking with?" She said.

"This is Sean, the guy you met at Ralph's yesterday."

"Oh hey Sean! I was wondering if you were going to call me."

"Yea, I didn't pump myself up to come speak with you to not call you. If I'm honest right now, I'm so nervous." I smacked myself in the forehead for blurting that out.

"Why are you nervous?" Andrea asked with a laugh.

"Well. . . I don't really know. I just don't want to call and turn you off for any reason. It may be hard to believe but I am no ladies man. This stuff doesn't come natural to me." I admitted, shaking my head at how much information I was giving so soon into the conversation. Andrea laughed so hard I could hear her covering her mouth.

"Oh now you're laughing at me. I don't know if that's good or bad." I said as I rubbed the back of my neck.

"It's not bad at all, you're so honest. That's refreshing to me." She said.

"It's not always a good thing, I'm honest sometimes to a fault. I stick my foot in my mouth a lot." I said.

Andrea laughed again then said, "Well this should be interesting."

"So tell me about yourself beautiful. Do you live in the area? Work nearby? " I asked.

"Keep calling me beautiful and you're gonna win yourself all kinds of points with me." She said.

"Okay beautiful, don't threaten me with a good time." I flirted.

"Well I live nearby, I just rented a small house, just big enough for me and my little maltese Sugar." She said.

"Oh you have a dog? I love Dogs. When I get a house with a backyard I'd love a Rottweiler."

"That's my favorite dog!" She said.

"Mine too. I always wanted one, but my mom was never into pets so all she let me have were goldfish." I said.

"Those surely aren't pets." She laughed.

"I know, I had to get a new one every other week, until I gave up on them." I laughed.

"Oh and to answer your other question. I own Uniquely Me. It's a boutique right across the street from Ralphs in that shopping center."

"Oh yea, I know exactly where that is."

"Yea it's my baby. I've only been open a year, but have been very successful" she said.

"Well congratulations! That's awesome!"

"Thank you! It hasn't been easy, but it's so worth it. And what do you do?" She asked.

"I'm a Pediatric Therapist over at Kaiser in LaBrea." I said

"Oh really? I'm very impressed. Handsome and smart." She said.

"I do what I can." I blushed.

We talked until about 3am. The conversation just flowed. I told her about my upbringing.

"My mom, Marsha raised me by herself. I never knew my dad, he skipped out on us before I was born. It had to be hard for her to do everything on her own. She worked two jobs just to make sure I had everything I needed."

"She sounds like a really good mom."

"She is. She's the best mom I could have ever asked for." I said, smiling thinking about my mom.

"She seems to have raised a really good son. She's probably all protective of you, being so handsome and all."

I loved giving compliments, but it was still very hard for me to take them.

I said without thinking,"Yea, I used to be ugly too. I mean like real ugly! Buck teeth, acne, bad haircut. . ."

"Bad haircut?" She laughed, "please explain that."

"Well my mom, trying to save money use to cut it, I got made fun of a lot for having a lopsided flat top." I shook my head at the thought.

Andrea tried her best not to laugh at me too hard.

"Yea, my cousin Shelby has been there for me through it all. She always stuck up for me. It wasn't until my senior year in high school when I got my braces off, and my face started to clear up, that I started to break out of my ugly shell. By then my mom was letting me go get my haircut by someone who knew what they were doing. That's when all the girls started to come sniffing around. I wasn't very confident, so although I had opportunity, it was rare that I took advantage of my new found popularity with the ladies. It wasn't until college when I met my best friend Eli that I started to come into my own a little more. Eli helped me gain more confidence. He's pretty wild and outgoing, being his homie always brought around the fine looking ladies." I said, feeling like I had divulged too much. "Now I'm rambling too much, tell me about you."

"Well, I was born in Louisiana. We moved to california when I was 2, so I don't really remember it. I have a brother who is a few years younger than me and a little sister who is 21. My parents have been married for 35 years and I'm very close with all of them." she told me.

I envied that. I always wanted siblings, but Shelby was as close to one as I would ever have.

"That's real cool. I always wanted siblings myself. And Louisiana, does that mean you're Creole like Beyonce?"

"Yea," She said laughing," Just like Beyonce. People rarely know what nationality I am. They always think I'm Puerto Rican."

"I knew you were a sista, no denying that."

"I'm not even going to ask you why you said it that way."

"Good because I didn't want to explain it." I said laughing, feeling like I dodged a bullet.

Her curves were definitely from African decent, and I didn't want to offend her by pointing out that I had noticed all that booty.

She told me about her best friend Jamie and how they had been inseparable since high school. Their relationship sounded a lot like the one I had with Eli. I learned that she went to UCLA for college and majored in business. Not only was she beautiful but she was smart. UCLA is not an easy school to get into. I found out she was single, and had been for quite some time. That made my insides jump, because I knew I had a chance. We never got into past relationships. I figured it was too soon to talk about that, and I didn't have many to speak of anyway.

She was so easy to talk to, and her voice was so soothing. I could listen to it forever, but I could sense her getting tired.

"Andrea, I know you're probably exhausted. I didn't mean to keep you up this late." I said.

"It's okay sweetie, I'm enjoying talking to you. I am tired though. I haven't been up this late in a long time." She said with a yawn.

"Oh I'm sweetie now huh?" I said with a smile.

"Yep. I just call em like I see em." She said.

"Okay, I like that. Even though I don't want to, I'm gonna let you go Beautiful." I said.

"I'm gonna take you up on that. We'll be talking until the sun comes up if I don't get off the phone now." She said through another yawn.

"Well do you think I can see you tomorrow after work? Maybe grab a bite to eat?" I asked, hoping she would agree.

"That sounds like a plan. How about we grab some Bayou Grill over there on LaBrea? Sounds like it's local to both of us." She suggested.

"I love that place. Then it's a date! 6:30?"

"Sounds excellent. I'll meet you there at 6:30."

"Until then, you have a great day." I said.

"You too sweetie."

I laid in my bed smiling as I fantasized about Andrea. I drifted off to sleep with that beautiful girl on my mind.

Andrea

I stayed up talking on the phone to Sean until 3am. I can't remember the last time I was up that late on the phone with anyone; let alone a good looking man. I'm smitten with him, but I tried my best not to let on to the fact. A sista can't play all her cards at once. I know better than that.

I was so tired when I got to the boutique, and Ashlynn could tell.

"What's wrong with you today Drea? Had a long night?" Ashlynn asked.

"Nothing wrong, was just up most of the night." I smiled.

"Ew doing what!?" Ashlynn said.

"I wasn't having any coochie coo time if that's what you're thinking." I laughed.

"Ugh , that's exactly where my head was." Ashlynn said with a laugh.

"No I was on the phone all night with that guy I was telling y'all about yesterday, Sean." I smiled.

"Ohhh. . . sooo. . .what were y'all chatting about all night?" She asked, batting her eyes at me.

"Everything really. We touched on so many things. I felt like I've known him forever. If my tiredness didn't take over we would have been on the phone until the sun came up." I smiled

"Wow he's got you beaming!"

"I told you he was different." I said, smiling at the thought of him.

"OK give me some details, don't leave me hanging Drea."

"Well, for starters, he's sweet as hell. He gives lots of compliments. He also has a great sense of humor. We laughed so much my cheeks started to hurt."

"Aww ain't that cute."

"Don't try and clown me Ash, I think I have a crush on him already."

"How old are you again? A crush?" Ashlynn said laughing.

"You just don't understand, you're still into knuckleheads and thugs. You'd turn your nose up at a guy like Sean."

"You're probably right about that. I like my guys with a little street in them. Both in the streets and in the sheets if you know what I mean." Ashlynn said, thrusting her pelvis in my direction.

"That's more than I EVER needed to know about you Ash, you're too much!" I said laughing.

"So when are you going to see him?" Ashlynn asked.

"After we leave here I'm going to meet up with him at the Bayou Grill."

"Oh! Can I come!? I want some shrimp! And I need to see what all the hype is about with this Sean character."

"How about no! I know how you get. You'll be all up in his grill asking him questions and flirting before we even get a chance to sit down good."

"I won't I promise!" Ashlynn begged.

"You will and the answer is still no!"

Before I left work, I called up Jamie. She ran a children's dance studio in Culver City. She was able to teach classes and keep Bella with her while Giselle went to Kindergarten during the day. I needed to tell her about last night and hopefully have her calm my nerves about this date with Sean.

"Drea girl!" She said.

"J!" I said as soon as I heard her voice. "I have to tell you what happened!"

"Is this about that guy? What happened? He do something already?"

"Well yea, he did. He's awesome girl! I talked to him for hours on the phone last night. I really like him. I'm about to meet up with him at Bayou Grill."

"Damn he don't waste no time does he!" She said with a giggle.

"Nope, he made me feel so comfortable. I felt like I had known him forever by the time we hung up last night." I said, beaming.

"Well I'm happy he seems like a good guy so far. I'm gonna have to meet him though, you know I got to see for myself."

"I know, if all goes well, hopefully, you'll be meeting him soon."

"Ok cool. Well relax pooh, have some fun tonight."

"I'll try my best to relax. I am really buggin out. It's been a long time since I liked someone this much." I confessed.

"I know girl! I been around for them all. Well my class is starting soon. Call me and let me know how things went."

"Okay babes, I will. Love ya J!"

"Love ya too Drea."

I couldn't wait to meet up with Sean after work. This morning, I made sure I put on my favorite jeans, the ones that hugged my ass ever so nicely. I grabbed one of our new tops that had just come in off the rack, a teal off the shoulder sweater. I looked cute and sassy without coming off like I was trying too hard.

The place where we were meeting was just a few blocks away from my boutique. After I told Ashlynn she couldn't tag along for the last time, after all her begging, she knew I meant it. I closed the boutique, hugged baby sis and hopped in my car. I checked my face in my mirror a few times before I turned the car on. I had never been this nervous to meet up with anyone.

"You need to chill Andrea, snap out of it!" I said to myself aloud.

I pulled up to the restaurant and saw Sean pull up right behind me in a really nice black truck. I sat there for a few seconds before I got out, trying to shake the nervousness I was feeling. When I climbed out of my car, Sean was standing next to my door holding his hand out to help me. I accepted his hand, and locked up my car.

"I thought I was gonna beat you here. " I blushed.

"I like to be prompt, especially for a beautiful woman." He said, smiling that sexy smile of his.

"Oh are we flirting already?" I said with a wink.

"You might as well get used to that now, the flirting will be non-stop from here on out." He said, winking back.

"Oh ok, I see." I said.

Noticing we were still holding hands, I slid my hand from his, pretending like I needed something from my purse. I was suddenly very aware of how touchy feely he was with me, and even more aware that I was allowing it. Once we were inside, Sean found us a table. He pulled my chair out for me, scoring a few extra points for being a gentleman.

"Do you know what you want? I'll go up and order us something" Sean said.

" Umm. . . I think I want the red snapper and shrimp meal with a side of dirty rice." I said.

"Ok, you sure you can eat all of that?" He asked, eyebrows raised.

"Have you seen these hips!? I can chow down with the best of em." I said with a laugh. Sean smiled as he walked to the counter to place our order. I knew I shouldn't have said anything about my hips. Sean kept looking back at me and I knew he was trying to see what I was working with. He came back to the table a minute later and sat across from me.

"They'll bring the food over when it's ready." He said.

"Ok cool. So how was your day? Explain to me what you do again."

"It was pretty good, I'm a Pediatric Therapist. I work with kids from babies on up to 18. I just make it a really comfortable environment for the kids to talk to me about whatever they need to." he said with a smile.

"That sounds very interesting. I love kids. I have a nephew, He's 2."

"I have a one year old Cousin-Godson."

"Cousin- Godson? I said, with a puzzled look.

"Yea, he's my cousin Shelby's son. I got knighted with the GodFather title after she found out she was pregnant."

"Oh nice, someone trusts you enough to assign you that title huh?" I said with a raised eyebrow and a smile.

"Oh yea, I'm kind of the man!" He said, flashing me his pearly whites again. I found myself blushing a lot. I tried to hide it, but my fair skin wasn't letting me play it off.

Our food came and we continued to talk and laugh for what seemed like hours. I was enjoying the groove we had fallen into. It was comfortable and I was able to relax.

"My boy Eli would be pleased to see me out with such a fine looking woman. He has been clowning me for weeks for not talking to you before now."

"Before now? We just met though." I said, raising an eyebrow.

"Yea we just met, but I've been wanting to meet you for awhile now." he confessed. He explained how he saw me months ago at Ralphs, but couldn't get up the nerve to speak to me after I smiled at him that day.

"You did look kind of familiar," I said, tilting my head looking at him through squinted eyes.

"You don't remember, quit playin'!" He said with a laugh.

"You're right, I don't." I confessed with a giggle."My mom always told me to try and be kind and smile at everyone. I could be making their day with that small act of kindness. " Sean stared at me smiling,"Your mom is right, you made my day with your smile all those months ago."

"My little sister wanted to come with me today," I said, changing the subject. All that staring he was doing was starting to get too intense. "But I told her no. She can be a mess."

"You should have let her come." He said.

"Nope! No way in hell."

"Why not?" He chuckled.

"Because she is too much. I would have been so embarrassed by her line of questioning." I said shaking my head at the thought.

"What would she have asked, I need to be prepared for when I meet her." He said

"She would have been all up in your face. Asking if you are married, have kids, been to jail, were gay..."

"No, nope, nope and HELL NO!" He laughed.

"When you meet Jamie, prepare for something similar except she won't try to flirt with you." I laughed.

"Oh WHEN I meet Jamie huh? We're planning for the future already?" He said with a wink.

I blushed so hard I felt my face get hot.

"I won't even let you meet Eli, his dog ass would try and steal you from me for sure," he said.

"Steal me from you huh?" I said teasing him.

Sean smiled really hard and looked away. We had both been caught talking about the future. This was going to be interesting.

Sean was very easy going and I felt so comfortable with him. It was a little scary for me to feel that way with someone so soon.

I kept thinking,"He's different. And in the best possible way"

Sean

I was in awe of Andrea as I sat across from her. She was beautiful, and smart, and could hold a conversation. We talked until we were the last 2 people in the place. I saw the look that the girl at the register was giving, one that said, "wrap it the hell up so I can go the hell home." I excused myself so I could ask the girl at the register for 2 boxes. She handed them to me with a roll of her eyes. I took them and smiled.

"What was her deal?" Andrea asked.

"Oh nothing, she just hates life and us laughing and carrying on is killing her softly." I said.

"Oh lord." Andrea said loudly, glancing over at the girl at the register, then bursting into a fit of laughter.

"You better stop it before she comes over here and jumps on the both of us." I told her.

"I'm sorry, I'm soo sooo sorry." Andrea said between tears and giggles.

"Let pack this food up and head out." I suggested.

"OK sweetie pie, let's do it." She said.

We got the food together and I helped Andrea up from the table. She wasn't lying about those hips. I had seen them before, but up close and in those jeans, I could hardly stop myself from staring. We both waved at register girl and headed outside. It was dark as we stood under a street light near our cars.

"So listen Andrea, I'm really having a great time with you, and I kind of don't want it to end." I said, hoping she felt the same.

"It doesn't have to yet. It's only 8:30. We could go around the corner to my house. I only live 2 blocks from here." She suggested.

"That would be great, you really don't mind?"

"I wouldn't have suggested it if I did silly." She said with a sweet smile.

CHAPTER THREE

SEAN

I followed Andrea the 2 blocks to her house. It was a nice little house on a quiet block. It had a cute little picket fence around it, and nice colorful flowers in the flower bed near the porch. The grass was neatly manicured. It looked like a home.

"Nice house." I said, as I walked behind her up the 3 stairs.

"Thanks. I really like it." She said as she opened the door.

As soon as the door opened, her Maltese Sugar came running to up. She ran right past Andrea and up to me. I picked her up and scratched behind her ears. Sugar licked my nose.

"Whoa, whoa Sugar! I like you too, but I don't get down with dog kisses." I said as I put Sugar back on the floor.

Andrea laughed that cute little laugh.

"Sugar! Now you know you're supposed to save all those kisses for mama!" she giggled. Sugar came over and licked Andrea's toes.

"Y'all are into some kinky ish I see." I said with a laugh.

"Don't be jealous. Take your shoes off, she'll be all on your feet too." she laughed.

"I'm good. I don't even know her like that yet."

"You don't know what you're missing. Have a seat, I'll be right back. You need anything?" She asked.

"No, I'm okay. You just hurry back before I get lonely in here by myself." I said with a smile.

"You'll be alright. I'll send Sugar back in there to keep you company." She laughed as she went down the hall.

I looked around her living room. It was much nicer than my place. There were a few pictures hanging up on the wall. A picture of her family stood out the most. Her mom could pass for her older sister. She was beautiful too. I figured the guy and girl in the picture were her siblings. Andrew looked like someone you don't want to fuck with and Ashlynn, she was a pretty girl, but had nothing on Andrea. Next to the family picture was one of Andrea and a woman I assumed was Jamie. She was a pretty chocolate girl with a short bob type haircut. I see Andrea only surrounded herself with beautiful people.

A minute later, Andrea walked back in the room. She had taken off the outfit she was wearing and put on some sweats and a tank top.

"I thought I told you to have a seat with your nosey self." She said with a chuckle.

"I saw your fine mama over there and I couldn't help but to look." I said with a smile. Andrea punched me in shoulder playfully.

"Don't make me call my daddy." She said with a smile.

"I'm not messing with your pops, he looks like he don't play!" I said.

"He don't, you just remember that!" She said with a grin.

We walked over to the sofa and sat down. We chatted some more about her boutique and her family. I guess she was feeling comfortable with me, she started to tell me things most people would withhold for awhile, not divulge on a 1st date. She talked a lot about Andrew. She said they were very close and they hung out whenever they could. Apparently Andrew's son Tylor was by his ex-girlfriend who was cheating at the time the baby was conceived.

"That's some Maury type stuff right there. In the case of baby Tylor, Andrew. . ."

"I know right!" She said with a laugh.

"Well I do hope that's his child, I couldn't even imagine what he's going through. That's why I'm very careful with my junk."

"Geez don't call it junk. Like you just take it off and toss it aside." she said, shaking her head.

"I'm just sayin'…"

"You just saying nothing." She said with a smirk.

At that moment I had the strongest urge to kiss her. We made eye contact, and I think she knew what was on my mind.

"So. . ." she said. trying to avoid my gaze.

"So. . ." I said, grabbing her hand, interlocking our fingers.

Andrea blushed so hard I could feel the heat radiated through her body. I wanted to feel more of it. I scooted closer to her.

"You truly are a beautiful woman Ms. Andrea, one of the most beautiful I've ever seen." I told her sincerely.

"Thank you. You're not so bad yourself Mr. Sean. You're actually quite handsome." She said, blushing more.

"Stop, you're gonna make a black man blush." I said, smiling at her.

Andrea grinned and put her head on my shoulder. I kissed her forehead and stroked her hair. She let out a sexy sigh that sent chills up my spine. I shifted my position, and Andrea looked up at me.

"You okay?" She asked.

"As okay as I'm gonna be around someone as mmm as you." I said.

"As Mmm as me? What does that mean?" she said with a smile.

"You know, like campbell's soup." I said.

Andrea laughed a sweet laugh and scootered a little closer to me. I felt myself getting hot. I wanted to make a move, but I didn't want to press my luck. I let my hand slide from her curls down to her thigh. She didn't move away, so I took that as a sign that it was okay with her.

"What's your favorite flower?" I asked.

"Lilies. Purple lilies." She said.

"Great choice. "

"Why'd you ask?"

"Mind your business."

"Oh, like that? Okay." She said with a grin.

"Yep." I said scooting her even closer to me

"What's your last name?" She asked randomly.

"Williams." I said, "What's yours?"

"LaSalle."

"Now it's official. Once you know people's last names, that's when shit gets real." I said.

"Well I guess shit just got real." she said with a giggle.

I let myself relax as we chatted a little more. Andrea relaxed too. She was curled up on me with her head on my shoulder. I had taken my shoes off and had sunken down into the corner of the sofa. I traced circles on her thigh. She did the same on my abs.

I was feeling comfortable and brave so I asked, "Andrea, can I do something I've been wanting to do for awhile?"

"What's that?"

I pulled her to me and softly kissed her lips.

she looked at me and smiled.

"Wait...do that again." She said looking at me like she couldn't remember what had just happened.

I pulled her in, and slowly kissed her again. I felt her lips part, and I took that as an open invitation. Our tongues danced a perfect waltz. My breathing matched hers as I followed her lead. I pulled her all the way on top of me so that she was straddling me, knowing she would feel my erection; I wanted her to. She let out a slow moan as I gripped her ass with both hands. I found a spot she liked right below her ear lobe. She let out a sound that let me know I should keep going. She began to grind her hips on top of me, and I felt my erection grow.

"You're gonna get yourself in trouble." She whispered in the sexiest voice.

"I like this kind of trouble." I whispered back, kissing her neck.

I slid my hands up the front of her shirt slowly, her erect nipples on my fingertips. She let out a loud gasp, biting her bottom lip. The look she gave me let me know she wanted exactly what I wanted; for me to be inside of her. I slid her shirt off, and tossed it to the side. She straddled me, kissing my lips sweetly. I gripped both of her breasts, kissed, sucked, and flicked my tongue over her right nipple, then the left. Her full C cups were perfect.

Andrea stood up, and looked at me with her head tilted biting her bottom lip. I could tell she was contemplating something.

"What's the matter beautiful? Too fast? Too soon? You want me to leave?" I asked, starting to stand up.

"Nothing is wrong, I just don't want to move too fast. I don't want you thinking I'm an easy girl. But I have to be honest, I'm wanting you bad right now." She said twirling a curl, looking me in the eyes.

"I don't want you to do anything you don't wanna do. All of this is on your terms, but I want you bad too. Can't you tell?" I ask, glancing down at my manhood.

She smiled that sexy smile and grabbed me by the hand. I stood willing to follow her wherever she took me. She lead me down the hall to her bedroom.

Andrea

The last thing I want Sean thinking is that I just bring men home and sleep with them. We hadn't talked about it, but I've been celibate for over a year. He had turned my oven on, and I don't want to turn it off. We might as well cook. I just don't want to ruin whatever this is by giving up the cookie too soon. But hell, we're adults here, so, fuck it.

I lead Sean to my bedroom. It's full of shades of purples and beige. Not tacky though. Classic and classy thank you very much.

"Nice room." Sean said.

"Thank you, I'm sure you can tell what my favorite color is." I said smiling

"Yep, purple everythang." He said with a smile

I could tell he was just as nervous as I was. The small talk was just to break the ice.

"So Sean, When was the last time you had sex?" I asked matter of factly.

"Well to be honest it's been awhile, Maybe a year or so." He said honestly

"Really? Your choice?" I asked, smiling at him.

"Yes my choice, who else's choice would it be?" He said with a laugh.

"I'm just saying, that's a long time for a man."

"Well how long has it been for you?"

"The same actually."

"By choice?" He asked with a grin.

"Yes by choice." I laughed.

"Well good, now that we've gotten that out of the way. . ."

Sean came and stood in front of me. He was wearing a black V-neck t-shirt and jeans. I helped him take his shirt off, and unbuttoned his pants. The whole time he never took his eyes off of me. I felt myself get hot all over. Sean walked me over to my bed. He slid my sweats off and got on his knees. He looked up at me, and licked his lips. He slid my thong off with his teeth. When we got to my inner thigh I felt my body shudder.

Sean rubbed his hands up and down my legs slowly. I was so happy I shaved that morning. He moved up to my thighs and rubbed my butt, and slid his hands between my legs. His fingers grazed my love slightly and a moan escaped my lips. He looked up at me, smiling. He let his fingertips slightly tease my love over and over, he was digging the reaction he was getting from me.

He hit a sweet spot and my knees buckled.

"Wetness." He said smirking at me,"Did I create all that?"
"I think you did. What are you gonna do about it?"
"I can show you much better than I can tell you."

Sean laid me down on my bed. He kissed me from my lips, to my neck, and down to my breasts. He stayed there for a minute and explored. He moved down to my stomach, and kissed down to my love. He gently kissed my clit and without warning he was in a thigh lock.

"Sorry." I said, embarrassed. Here we are having sexy time, and I'm trying to kill this man before we can even reach the promise land.
"Just relax baby, I'm gonna take care of you, I promise." He said. I trusted his word and let myself fully relax.
He nibbled on each thigh as I moaned and squirmed. He moved back up to my love and feasted on me like I was his last meal. His tongue kissing, sucking, teasing every inch. He reached a hand up and massages my breasts as he continued to feast. I could hardly contain myself. I got loud and didn't care who heard my extasy.

"Oh Sean baby, you're gonna make me cum!"
"Mmm hmmm!"
"You feel so good!"
"Mmmm hmmm!"
"Right there, right there! Don't stop!"

"mmm hmmm!"

Moments later I had climaxed was all over the bed. It had been so long since I felt anything like that, and Sean was by far the best at it.

"Damn Sean. I wasn't expecting that." I said as I tried to catch my breath.
"I'm full of surprises." He said as he kissed my inner thigh.

Sean laid next to me with his eyes closed. I slid my hand down his chest until I reached his throbbing erection. I began to stroke it as he let out a soft moan. Long slow strokes up and down. I could feel his body tense. I watched his toes curl. I was getting just as turned on as he was.

I slid down to his waist, and kissed his stomach. Sean was built like a Ken doll with his clothes off. I positioned myself between his thighs. He opened his eyes, looking at me. I smiled sweetly as I took him into my mouth. I licked around the tip for a while, then kissed down the length of it. He had a nice size on him. I was impressed. I tongue kissed it over and over. His moans grew louder, as his body got tense. I heard him say, " Damn baby" Over and over. His reaction was turning me on and making me kiss, suck, lick tease him even more.

"you're gonna make me cum babe."
"mmm hmmm!"
"That feels so damn good!"
"Mmmhmm!"

Sean grabbed my hair and pulled at it ever so gently, then harder. I felt the wetness between my legs become hot. Who knew that hair pulling was a turn on for me. The more he tugged the more I felt myself close to climax again. He tugged, moaned, moved his hips.

"I'M CUMM. . . ."

Sean climaxed and let out a caveman style grunt. I stroked his love until his body relaxed. I grabbed a few tissues off my nightstand and wipe my hands. I laid next to him on my bed.

"That was intense." he said wiping sweat from his forehead.

"It was, I climaxed that time too."

"From doing that to me?"

"Yep, you made me enjoy it."

"You're awesome, will you marry me?" he said with a smile.

"Get me a ring first." I said, smiling back.

"I'm on it." Sean said extending his hand for a high five.

"It was that good I get a high five?" I asked extending my hand.

"I'd give you two, but I don't have enough energy, you stole most of it."

"I'll give you a moment to get some of it back." I said with a devilish grin.

We laid there caressing each other, my legs on top of his. We stared at each other for what seemed like forever.

"You got condoms?" I asked.

"No, I haven't had sex in forever. I don't just walk around with them." he said with a laugh.

"I might have some somewhere." I said, getting up to go check.

I know I bought some a while ago. A woman has to always be prepared. I went to my nightstand to check the drawers. I fumbled around in there for awhile before I found a single golden Magnum. I was shocked it wasn't expired.

> "Found one!" I announced. Holding it in the air like I had just won a prize.
> "No pressure." He said with a smile.
> "None at all. You have to be comfortable too" I told him.
> "I am. It's been awhile though."
> "Don't worry sweetie, we're in the same boat."

I handed Sean the condom. I scooted over to him and licked and sucked his bottom lip. I slide my tongue in his mouth and our tongues danced around for awhile. He laid me on my back and began to tease my body with licks, sucks and nibbles of his own. We were both hot again. I stroked his love a few times, before he slid the condom on.

Sean positioned himself between my legs and rested on top of me.

> "Be gentle with me. It's been awhile. I still want to be able to walk in the morning." I said.
> "I will, Don't worry. I told you I'm gonna take care of you." He said with a smile as he kissed my lips.

I relaxed my hips and let him inside of me. I let out a gasp, tensed up, and then relaxed. My wetness and tightness coupled with his thickness and hardness was a perfect combination. We started out slowly, my slow grind matching his thrust. Each movement felt like heaven. I knew it had been a while for me, but the way he felt was magical. I requested him to move harder and faster. He followed directions well.

"Turn over." He whispered.

I complied.

I propped myself up on my knees and elbows. Sean grabbed my waist and slid himself inside of me. I backed it up on him like it was the last song of the night. I felt myself ready to climax and slowed my motion.

"Lay on your side." Sean said with a smirk.

I complied.

I laid on my side and Sean lifted my right leg, putting it over his shoulder and slid inside of me. This was a new position for me, but it was the best one yet. Within a minute I felt myself on the verge of climax. Without warning I was coming again and so was he. He stroked until his love had run out. He collapsed beside me without removing himself from me. I felt his convulse and throb inside of me, while I felt myself tighten around him. He slowly slid himself out of me making sure he held onto the condom.

"Where's the bathroom?" He asked.
"Just outside the door."

He got up and flushed the condom in the toilet.

"You wanna snuggle with me?" I asked as he reentered the room.

"I thought you'd never ask, I was sure you were gonna just kick me out." he said with a smile.

I reached for his hand and pulled him down onto the bed. He scooted close to me and assumed the spooning position. We were both relaxed. For me it felt natural like a puzzle piece firmly in position.We cuddled up and I dozed off with a smile on my face.

Andrea

"I can't believe you fucked him on the first date!" Jamie said, taking a sip of her frappuccino.

"I didn't plan on it. It just kind of happened." I told her, taking a sip of mine.

"You could have at least waited a few dates. What happened to the 8 date rule?"

"That kind of went out of the window when he kissed this spot right here," I said, my body shivering as I pointed to the spot on my neck with Sean's name written all over it.

"Damn, what was that!? An aftershock?" Jamie asked smiling at me. A smile which turned into a belly laugh. The girl had tears running down her face and everything.

"Jamie don't do me like that. This is my life here." I said trying to keep my face serious.

Jamie stared at me a second before we both broke into fits of laughter.

People in Starbucks started to stare at us. We had to pull it together.

Jamie said,"Damn what y'all looking at!? We can't laugh? My sister got some penis last night!"

I turned red and put my head on the table. Jamie kept laughing.

"Excuse her everyone, she didn't take her meds today." I said dragging a laughing Jamie out of there.

"Ok, ok, I'm sorry Drea. I couldn't help myself. "

" Yea you could have, you just have no sense." I said smiling at her, shaking my head.

"So have you heard from him yet today?" Jamie asked, wiping her eyes.

"Not yet, but it's still early." I said, silently wondering why I hadn't heard from Sean. I hoped sleeping with him so soon hadn't ruined what we were starting.

"You know I'm only clowning Drea. Y'all are grown people, so sex shouldn't ruin anything if it's real." Jamie said, putting her arm around my neck.

She was right. If Sean was just in it to hit it and quit it, then I was better off anyway.

Sean

I left Andrea's house this morning in the best mood ever. We were snuggled up so good, I didn't hear my phone's alarm when it started to go off. I had 10 minutes to get to work once I woke up. I rushed to put on my clothes, kissed Andrea on the forehead and was on my way to my place. I had to shower and change clothes before I got to the hospital.

I walked around all day with my head in a cloud. I even called the nurse in our reception area Andrea twice. I'm sure everyone could see that I was happy.

I didn't have free time until after work. I couldn't wait to call Andrea. I got into my truck and dialed her number.

"Hey beautiful." I said as soon as she answered the phone.

"Hey Sean." She said, no smile in her voice.

"What's wrong Andrea? You don't sound so happy to hear from me."

" I am, I've been thinking about you all day. It just that..."

"It's just that what?" I asked, concerned.

"It's just that I don't know if I made the right choice last night. I mean it was great. You are great, but I don't want to mess anything up by throwing sex in the mix too soon." She said, honestly.

I understood where she was coming from, but I'm not that guy. I wasn't only with her just to get the coochie. She was so much more than that. I needed to reassure her.

"Andrea, I hope you don't think I'm with you just for sex. It's way more than that for me. I really like you a lot and I hope we can continue whatever this is we're starting."

"I want to continue it too," she said; her voice smiling like I had become used to.

"Well would you mind continuing it as my girlfriend?" I asked, hoping it didn't sound childish.

"Your girlfriend? You asking me to be your girlfriend?" She said with a giggle.

"I am, what do you think about that?"

"Okay, I guess I have a boyfriend then." She said.

"I guess you do." I said smiling.

We made plans to see each other later. I couldn't believe had a girlfriend, that Andrea was MY girlfriend.

CHAPTER FOUR

Sean

I had been seeing Andrea for a few weeks, and things were going great between us. I took her to meet Shelby and they hit it off like they had known each other forever. Even Justin loved her. He toddled after her everywhere she went. Andrea just has that effect on people.

I even introduced her to Eli, against my better judgement. Eli was impressed. He flirted with her just like I had warned.

"I know you like my Bro and all, but I'm sure I look better than him right?" He said, slyly smiling at her.

"I mean, you're good looking Eli. You don't need me to tell you that." Andrea said, laughing.

"Okay, now that that's established, maybe you should come on over to the dream team." He said flexing his muscles.

"You know what," Andrea said, patting him on the back,"I think I'm good right where I am."

Andrea was good at deflecting his sly advances. He's not used to being turned down, not even when he's just joking around. After that meeting, Eli made sure to tell me I had done well.

"You hit that yet." he pulled me to the side to ask.

"Get out my damn business dude, ol nosey ass." I said, shaking my head at him. I was keeping that information to myself. I'd maybe save it for a later conversation, if I ever told him at all.

Andrea invited me to a BBQ at her parents house in Westchester. I was nervous as hell to meet everyone. She gave me the address and asked me to meet her there around 2. This should be interesting.

I walked up to the porch and rang the bell. It's a beautiful two story house in a quiet neighborhood. I wouldn't think any black people lived around here.

"Hey babe!" Andrea said, opening the door, kissing me on the lips.

"Hey beautiful." I said smiling at her.

"You brought flowers!" She said.

"No, They're for your mom with her fine. . ."

"Hey Drea who's at the door?" Her mom asked.

"Oh it's Sean mommy. He brought something for you."

"Oh he didn't have to do that." Mrs.LaSalle said smiling at me.

She took the flowers from my hands and hugged me with one hand around the neck.

"It's so nice to finally meet you." She beamed.

"It's nice to meet you too Mrs. LaSalle. I see where Andrea gets her beauty from." I said sincerely.

And beautiful she was. She was about the same height as Andrea. She was very fair skinned with reddish brown hair and the same curls and freckles as Andrea. She had hazel eyes that sparkled when she spoke. I could also see where Andrea got her shapely figure from. If Andrea is going to look half as good as her mom when she gets that age, and I'm still around, I'll be one lucky man!

"Show him to the backyard Drea."

"Thanks Mrs. LaSalle."

"Please, Call me Marie." she said, patting my shoulder..

"Okay Mrs. Marie." I said, wanting to smack myself for calling her Mrs. again.

"We'll work on that Mrs. business later, you're making me feel old," she joked.

"I'm sorry it's a habit."I told her, shaking my head at myself.

We got to the backyard where her dad Phil, brother Andrew, nephew Tylor, sister Ashlynn and her friend Jamie with her two girls and husband were sitting. Her dad and brother both looked at me and then at each other. If I wasn't nervous before, was nervous now.

"Everybody, this is Sean," Andrea announced.

Everyone waved at me. I waved back.

"Hey Sean." Ashlynn said with a wave and a smile.

"That's Ashlynn." Andrea said.

Ashlynn walked over and looked at me from head to toe and then back again. She smiled and I returned her smile.

"So. . .How YOU doin!?" Ashlynn asked.

"I'm good, how are you?" I asked.

"Much better now that I'm meeting the illustrious Sean." She said, looking at Andrea .

"Illustrious huh?"

"Yep, Drea talks about you ALL the time. I can hardly get her to shut up about you at work."

"That's not a bad thing is it?"

"Oh course not, I just know you must be putting it down because you got sista girl wide open!"

"Ashlynn!" Andrea yelled with flushed cheeks.

"What? What I do?" Ashlynn said trying to look innocent.

"Don't pay her any mind babe, she has absolutely no filter." Andrea said embarrassed.

Andrea pulled me away from Ashlynn so I could meet her dad and brother.

"Daddy this is Sean." Andrea said.

"Yes, Sean, I've heard a lot about you." Her dad said.

"I hope they were all good things Mr. LaSalle." I said nervous.

"Well of course. If they were bad things you'd have to wait out on the curb in your car." He said with a chuckle.

"Oh good. I've only heard great things about you guys too. Andrea always talks about her family and how close you guys are. " I said.

"Well I'm glad. My baby here hasn't brought a guy home since Ma. . ."

"Daddy!. . . Maybe you should go check on your meat before it burns." Andrea said, shooting her father a look.

"Oh. . oh yea, let me go do that. Nice meeting you Sean, we'll catch up in a bit." Her father said.

Andrea looked uneasy as she rubbed the back of her neck.

"You okay beautiful?" I asked.

"Yea, I'm fine. My daddy just gets to running his mouth a little too much. I have to cut him off sometimes so he doesn't say. . . So he doesn't ramble on."she said with an uncertain smile.

Just then her nephew ran over to us.

"Auntie Dre!" He said reaching up for her.

Andrea picked Tylor up and twirled him around.

"How's auntie's baby?" She asked him planting kisses on his cheeks.

"Fine." He said smiling at her.

"You been a good boy Ty?"

"I been good boy." He said cheesing

"Good. Auntie has a treat for you then."

"I like treats."

Andrea went over to the table and grabbed a package of bubbles.

"Here you go Ty. Auntie got you bubbles!"

"I LOVE bubbles!"

"I know baby. Go ask Auntie Ash to help you with them."

Tylor ran off in Ashlynn's direction.

"You're such a good aunt." I said.

"I try to be." She smiled.

Jamie pulled herself away from her husband and kids to come introduce herself. She was almost eye to eye with me. She wore a tank and cut off jean shorts that showcased her voluptuous figure. Her chocolate skin and light brown bob glowed in the sunlight.

"You must be Jamie." I said with a smile extending my hand.

"And you must be Sean." She said, extending her.

"Yep, it's really nice to meet you. Andrea calls you her second sister."

"Yea, that's my girl, we go way back. "

"Your little girls, they're gorgeous." I said, motioning toward her two little girls with their big fluffy curls and her same cocoa skin.

"Thank you, they are truly Divas." She said with a smile.

Jamie asked me 21 questions and I answered them all truly. She seemed to be impressed that I didn't hesitate once with anything she asked me.
She told Andrea," Okay girl, I think we can keep him. He passed my little interview."
Andrea smiled widely and grabbed my hand. Then her brother came over.

"Aye man! Wassup. I'm Andrew. I was waiting for my big head sister to introduce us but it looks like she was never gonna get to it." Andrew said as he shook my hand.

"Nice to meet you Bruh I'm Sean." I said shaking his hand.

"I've heard a lot about you man. Drea won't shut up about you." He said giving her a look.

"I can't shut up about her either. She's a great girl." I said smiling at Andrea.

"Y'all both making me sick right now."He laughed.

"I can't help it man, she's a keeper." I said putting my arm around Andrea's shoulder.

"Well if you're hanging around all day we'll catch up. I'ma go play with those bubbles with my boy. Drea you know those are my favorite!" He said playfully pushing her in the shoulder.

Andrew ran off to catch some bubbles, and I was able to relax. I had met the fam and they seemed to like me as much as I liked them.

"So. . . You can't stop talking about me huh?" I asked playfully.
"Shut up! I don't talk about you THAT much." Andrea blushed.

The BBQ went on and everyone was very welcoming. They shared stories like families do about their upbringing. Andrew told stories about his sisters when they were younger, embarrassing them both. Jamie told stories about her and Andrea in high school. She said she'd only tell the tame stories so her parents wouldn't freak out about it. We all laughed out loud and just had a nice comfortable time. I had been there 2 hours when we heard loud voices coming from the front of the house.

"That nigga knows it's his baby! I never told you he was yours Derrick! I don't even know why you followed me over here. You're such a fucking stalker!" A woman's voice yelled.
"Because that's my son! He looks just like me. I don't know why you playing this game. You know we were fucking around when you got pregnant. I want you, me and my son to be a family. I already called Maury!" A male voice said.
"Called Maury!? Nigga you is trippin'! I told you I'm not going on Maury! Ain't no need. I'm not about to make a fool of myself when I already know the truth. Nigga YOU can go on Maury by your damn self but me and my son won't be sitting up there with you."

Everyone in the backyard looked at Andrew all at the same time. He got up and stormed through the house out to the front.

"Kelly what the fuck is wrong with you!? Why are you even here!? You weren't invited. You know my mom and sisters can't stand you and they're all back there right now. You should leave and take this muthafucka with you!" Andrew said in a calm voice.

"Nigga who the fuck you think you talking to?" Derrick said stepping into Andrew's personal space.

"I'm talking to both of y'all! This is my parents house. Don't come over here disrespecting it." Andrew said.

"I told him not to follow me babe, he don't listen."Kelly said.

"First of all, don't call me babe, we ain't together no more. Second, I don't care what y'alls issue is, just get the fuck away from here with it." Andrew said.

We all heard the arguing. Andrea's dad jumped up and rushed to the front of the house with everyone following behind him.

"Y'all gon get off my property before I call the cops." Mr. LaSalle said.
"We are trying to have a peaceful day and you come around here trying to ruin it." Mrs. Marie said to kelly.

"I ain't here to ruin nothin'. I came to get my son." Kelly said.

"You knew I was going to bring him home this evening, and you could have called before you came over here." Andrew said

"Well I was already around here so I thought I should just come." Kelly said.

"Yeah, I wanted to see my son anyway." Derrick said looking at Andrew.

Before any of us knew it Andrew was in Derrick's face nose to nose. Mr. LaSalle had to get between them before a fight broke out.

"Mom please go grab Ty's things. He can go home with his mom since that's why she claims she's here." Andrew said.

Mrs. Marie went and grabbed the baby's bag and came back outside. She handed the stuff to Andrew.

"Here take his bag. I'll be back for MY SON next weekend." Andrew said, shooting a look at Derrick who was still being held by Mr. LaSalle.

Kelly took the bag and Tylor and walked to her car. Derrick walked to his car as well.

"I'll see y'all on Maury! I know that's my son and y'all ain't gon keep me from him." Derrick said as he got into his car

Andrea walked up to me with embarrassment written all over her face.

"I'm so sorry Sean. I didn't want you to be a witness to any of my family drama." She said, face red.

"It's okay. I'm just glad no one came to blows. It's not your fault. Doesn't look like it was any one here's fault."I told her.

"Yea Kelly is now, and always will be a bitch. It takes everything in me not to pull her glued in tracks out every time I see her. She did my brother wrong and she knows it. He doesn't deserve this at all." She said, her eyes welling up with tears.

"Don't cry babe, it's okay." I said, hugging her.

"I might have to talk Andrew into getting that paternity test after all." She said, looking around at her family.

Andrea

After that scene Kelly made at my parents house I needed to talk to Andrew. I had him come over my house the next day so we could discuss some things.

Andrew walked into my living room looking defeated. He looked out of sorts, his chocolate skin looking pale, short curly hair frizzy and undone, his hazel eyes dim like someone had turned the lights out. His 6'4" stocky frame slumped as he sat down on my sofa.

"Chip." I said, referring to the nickname I gave him growing up because I thought he was the same color as a chocolate chip.

"What's up Drea, what did you want to talk about?"

"I just needed to make sure you were okay after all that went down yesterday."

"I'm as good as I can be. We were having a great time before Kelly's ol dumb ass showed up."

"Yea we were, I'm sorry she had to ruin it."

"I'm sorry your boy Sean had to witness that. That's not the impression I wanted to leave on him."

"He was okay Chip. He wasn't turned off by it."

"Good, I really am sorry though."

"Don't be. It wasn't your fault."

"Well it kinda is, I fucked with Kelly without protection. I should have listened to people when they told me she was a hoe and all that." He said, digging his fists into the palm of his hand. He was becoming upset.

"We live and we learn Chip, but there is something I wanted to talk to you about."

"What's that?"

"I heard Derrick saying he called Maury."

"You don't think I'm going on that show, do you!?"

"No, no, but I do think maybe you should get the test done."

"Drea, Ty is my son. I've been the one taking care of him since the day he was born. I got a second job to make sure he had everything he needed." He said through clenched teeth and eyes that were beginning to water.

"I know that Chip, I have been there right along with you. You're a great father. Some men don't do even a quarter of what you do with and for Ty."

"I can't get that test done. What if it comes back that he's not mine? That would kill me." Andrew said, letting the tears fall.

"But you can't keep on like this. Derrick is not going to leave it alone. Kelly won't leave you alone either, since she's convinced he's yours." I told him, placing my hand on his shoulder.

"I hear what you're saying but my entire world would fall apart if he wasn't mine Sis. I don't think I could handle that." He said, full on sobbing now.

I embraced my brother. I had never seen him cry, not like this. I wrapped my arms around him and let him release it all into my shoulder. I rubbed his back, and at that moment I was just his big sister, and let him be my vulnerable baby brother.

A few days later, I took Andrew and Ty to get the paternity test. They told us it would be a few more days before the results would be back. Andrew got in contact with Derrick and told him to go submit a sample of his own, so that we could all find out once and for all. Derrick quickly agreed, since he was convinced that Ty was his.

After I dropped Andrew and Ty off, I went to meet Sean for lunch. I left Ashlynn running the boutique while I was gone.

We met up at Roscoe's Chicken and Waffles on Manchester. I was so happy to see him. He had become the bright spot on all of my days. I walked inside of the restaurant and spotted Sean sitting there smiling at me. Behind him I recognized a familiar face. My smile disappeared instantly.

"What's wrong babe?" Sean asked, as I made my way to the table.
"Nothing, I thought I saw someone I know."
"Who was it? Looks like you saw a ghost."
"Might as well have been."

I glanced over at the table in the corner and sure it enough, Mark was sitting there. He saw me notice him, and shifted his eyes back and forth, rubbing his neck a couple of times. I tried to become invisible, hiding my face behind my menu. I wished we'd picked a different place to eat.

"You know I've never really discussed my past relationships with you. I try not to live in the past, and I figured whatever happened with other women before me was none of my business."

"Yea I agree." Sean said, with a tilted head and raised eyebrow.

"Well my last real relationship ended pretty bad. My heart was broken into a million pieces by someone I really loved and trusted."

"I'm sorry babe, what brought this up though?"

"He's sitting right over there." I motioned with my head.

"Wow, what!?" Sean said looking in the direction I motioned.

"Yeah, I haven't seen him in a long time. I didn't know I'd feel like this if i ever saw him again." I admitted.

"And how do you feel?" Sean asked, concern in his eyes.

"Like I wanna go choke the life out of his ass!"

I gave Sean the cliff notes version of my relationship with Mark. Recounting some of the details made my palms sweat. I rubbed my brow trying to relax the lines I felt forming.

"Damn babe I'm sorry. That chump is up in here like its nothing." Sean said.

"Yea he's a coward. I can't stand his ass."

"Well you got me now, no need to even think about his punk ass again." He said, grabbing my hand and kissing it.

"You're right, I've been happier with you in these past few months than I ever was with him." I smiled, intertwining my fingers with his.

Sean leaned over to kiss me. I felt that familiar warmth inside that only he could give me.

Just then Mark walked over to our table.

"Hey Drea." He said, smiling.

"Andrea to you. What's up?"

"I saw you over here and just wanted to say hi. I've been back in cali a few months now. I called you, but you had changed your number."

"I could give two shits how long you've been back in cali. What are you even calling me for Mark? I have nothing to say to you."

"I wanted to apologize for the way things went down. I never meant to hurt you."

"Sure you didn't." Sean interrupted, he could tell I was getting upset.

In the process of going back a forth with Mark I forgot Sean was sitting there.

"Who is this clown." Mark said with an arrogant laugh.

"I'm her man, but you wouldn't know anything about being a man seeing how much of a coward you are. Oh and thank you for that. Your fuck up is my come up. She's the best prize." Sean said with a smile and a wink.

"Oh. . . uhh. . . yeah, whatever. You don't know shit about me. You don't know what we had!" Mark said, flaring his nostrils, cheeks getting flush.

"Obviously to you, y'all didn't have shit. And lower your got damn voice. I'm not some kid." Sean said shaking his head, amused by how upset Mark was becoming.

"You better get your boy Drea!" Mark said, glaring at Sean.

"You better keep it moving before you get your ass kicked . The truth hurts doesn't it." I said, glaring at Mark.

"Oh you gon let your boy fight me huh?" Mark asked looking at me, clenching his jaw.

"Nope, I won't let him put his hands on your trashy ass, I'd knock you out myself. Now get the fuck away from our table so we can enjoy our lunch." I told him, rolling my eyes so hard they could have gotten stuck.

Mark looked at me, with balled up fists, then at Sean, then back at me.

"Okay, you got it Drea, but if I see this fool again, no telling what will happen." Mark said, then he walking away. Leaving the few people in the place looking at the show we had just created.

"Yea okay bro. Keep it moving." Sean said raising his voice.

"Calm down sweetie. He isn't worth it." I assured him, patting his hand.

"But you are. I have to protect my lady."

"And that's why I Lo. . ."

"That's why you what?" Sean said raising an eyebrow, a smile creeping across his face.

"Nothing, let's change the subject." I said, my face becoming hot with embarrassment. I had almost let those three little words slip out. I ate them before they could escape.

Andrea

I couldn't believe that I almost told Sean I loved him the other day at lunch. More than that, I couldn't believe Mark's bold ass. I don't know why he didn't just walk out of there like he didn't see me. Mark getting all in Sean's face was uncalled for, but Sean standing up for me was sexy as hell. I was already in love with him, but that act of chivalry pushed me over the edge. It was hard for me to admit to myself that I was in love with Sean, I know for a fact that I don't want to be the first one to say it. I know that's childish, but that's just how I feel. With Mark, I told him first and we all know how that turned out. I felt like I needed to do things different this time around, so those words wouldn't cross my lips until he said it first.

Andrew is coming over today with his paternity results, that'll get my mind off of this love business for awhile. He wants me to open the results with him. On the phone he sounded so nervous. I assured him that either way the results read, we would deal with it.

"Drea come open the door." Andrew yelled through the screen.

"I'm coming hold your damn horses."

"Come on my guts are bubbling, I need to use your bathroom."

"You could have kept that to yourself. I might not open it now." I said with a laugh.

"Don't play Drea these results got me all fucked up. I might just shit all over your porch."

I opened the door, and Andrew ran right past me to the bathroom.

"Make sure you spray in there with yo nasty ass." I said, shaking my head.

"Shut up, this ain't funny."

"I know I'm sorry Chip. I'm just trying to lighten the mood. Finish your business in there. I'll be in the living room."

When Andrew finished, and came into the living room. He pulled the letter out of his back pocket and handed it to me.

"You sure you want me to do it?" I asked, looking up at him.

"Please." He said, sitting down.

As I opened the envelope I looked over at my brother. He didn't deserve anything but the best, and I hoped the contents of this envelope wouldn't put him in a bad space.

I slowly opened the envelope and pulled out the results. I read over them silently while Andrew stared at me. A slow smile crept across my face.

"He's yours Andrew! Ty is your son!" I shouted.

"Oh my God! Oh my God! Thank God!" Andrew shouted, tears streaming down his face.

"I'm so happy for you, for us, for all of us!" I said, hugging him.

"I can't believe this! I started to doubt it when Derrick said how much Ty looks like him. I almost believed he wasn't mine."

"I almost believed it too. I wished you didn't have to deal with Kelly, but we'll make it work."

"Drea thank you so much. Thank you for pushing me to do this. It was important, and I thank you so much for giving me strength." Andrew said hugging me tight.

"I love you Chip!"

"I love you too Drea."

CHAPTER FIVE

Sean

Me and Andrea have been dating for 4 months now. She is everything I wanted and needed her to be. She shows me what a woman really is, and I hope I was proving to her that I was a great man. I felt the time was right, I wanted her to meet my mom. I had never brought a woman home to meet mom, and I never wanted to bring any women home unless I was really serious about her. This was my longest relationship, and the first relationship with someone I knew had no ulterior motive. I had been talking about Andrea with mom,

"When will I get to meet this girl who is stealing my baby from me?" She would ask.

"soon mom, very soon." I would assure her.

On a Sunday morning I picked Andrea up and we made the 40 minute Drive to Van nuys. Andrea's boutique is closed on Sundays so it was perfect.

We pulled up to the house where I grew up. It still looked exactly the same. A small beige house, with the perfectly manicured lawn, and porch swing I helped mom install still sturdy.

"This is a sweet little house, reminds me of mine." Andrea said, as I helped her out of the passenger side.

"It holds lots of great memories."

"I bet it does." Andrea said squeezing my hand.

Mom heard the car door close and came outside to meet us.

"So this must be Andrea, She's so much prettier than you described baby." Mom said, winking at Andrea.

"I could never do her justice." I said, smiling.

"Thank you, Ms. Williams. You're even more beautiful than Sean said too. He always says I'm the most beautiful woman he's ever met next to you." Andrea said.

Mom looked at me and blushed. She hugged us both and lead us inside. There was a man sitting at the kitchen counter. He looked familiar to me, but I couldn't place where I knew him from.

"Sean, this is Michael." Mom said looking me straight in the eyes.

"Nice to meet you Michael." I said, looking at him. I was trying to figure out why mom had never introduced us before. She usually tells me everything.

"Nice to meet you too son." He said.

I turned and looked at Andrea who had a puzzled look on her face, then at mom who was smiling.

"Uh. . . will you guys excuse us, I need to have a word with my mom." I said, leading her into the living room.

"What's the matter baby?" Mom said, rubbing my shoulders.

"Mom, what's going on? I didn't know you had company. I didn't even know you were seeing anyone. Who is that in there?"

"Have a seat baby." Mom said, leading me to the couch.

"Okay," I said, sitting down."What's up mom?"

"Baby, Michael is your father." She said, placing her hands on top of mine.

I sat there stunned as she explained to me what my father, who I've never met was doing in her kitchen.

"Well baby, we got together in high school and when I found out I was pregnant with you, I told him. After that, I never saw or heard from him again. It turns out his parents had sent him to live with his grandparents down south, when they found out he had a child on the way. They didn't want him throwing his life away trying to raise a child at 17. He said he tried to contact me many times, but was unsuccessful. He got in contact with your Aunt Linda, she gave him my number. We spoke on the phone a few times and caught up. Michael showed up this morning out of the blue wanting to see me and to meet you. I decided not to tell you, I thought you wouldn't show up if I told you he was going to be here."

My mind was blown. I picked my chin up off the floor long enough to say, "Mom you could have told me he was going to be here. I wouldn't have brought Andrea. How does this look, me meeting him for the 1st time while you meet her for the first time."

"Don't get upset baby. I thought this was the best way." She said, squeezing my hand.

"I think you could have come up with a better way mom." I told her.

"Well it's happening now. You gonna leave?"

"No, I'm gonna stay, but I don't know that man. You never talked about him. I don't even know what to say to him." I said, head hanging in my hands.

"I named you after him. His full name is Michael Sean. Just be you, he wants to get to know you, just give him a chance."

Me and mom walked back into the kitchen to find Andrea and Michael chatting. She was doing what she always does, making everyone feel comfortable. I loved that about her. I stood next to Andrea, she grabbed my hand, smiling up at me.

"Everything okay?" She asked.

"Yea, I guess." I told her, kissing her forehead.

"Well Miss Andrea, let us girls go sit out front and chat." Mom said, grabbing Andrea's hand as they headed for the porch swing.

I stood in the kitchen staring at Michael. I now knew why he looked so familiar to me. We had the same face, same athletic build, same chocolate complexion and the same brown eyes. His graying hair showed his age, but aside from that, he was a mirror image of me. I stared at him for what seemed like forever.

"You okay son?" He asked.

"Yea. . . yea I'm alright." I said,

"I know this is strange and sudden. I don't mean to intrude on your life like this, but I have never stopped thinking about you. I heard through the grapevine that your mother had had a son and I was overjoyed."

"Is that right?"

"It is. I know it may be hard to believe, but I always wanted to be a part of your life. My parents made that impossible." he said, looking down, rubbing the back of his neck.

"So I heard." I said, conscious of my growing scowl.

"Both of them have passed on now, but I know they would have loved to know you." He said, sounding sincere.

"Well tell me, since you weren't here for my upbringing, what have you been doing with you life?" I asked, tasting the bitterness of my words.

"I wish I could have been here. After I was moved to Texas in my senior year, and couldn't find your mother, I enlisted in the army. I just retired last year. I've been all over the world, but I never stopped thinking about you or your mom. She was my first love, my last love."

"What do you mean your last love?" I asked, looking him in the eyes.

"I've never found anyone else that I was in love with. I felt guilty all these years for not being there for her. . . and you." He said, returning my stare.

I didn't know what to say. I wanted to be angry, but I just couldn't find it in myself. For whatever reason, I believed what he was telling me. I had grown up with the best mom anyone could ask for. She took care of me to the best of her ability. She made sure I could talk to my uncle Donny if there were "man things" I needed to know, that she had no knowledge of. Mom always made sure I felt loved and cared for and was never lacking. She made sure I didn't miss growing up without a dad. But, I never could shake the feeling that I was missing something. The longing I always felt on my birthday, Christmas or on Father's day when everyone else in school was making cards for their dads.

"Look Michael, I believe what you're telling me, but you have to understand how strange this is. I've never laid an eye on you a day in my life. It's gonna take some time to adjust. Michael looked at me with tears in his eyes.

"Just give me a chance to get to know you, That's all I ask son, that's all I want." He said, wiping his tears.

"I can give you that. It'll just be on my terms." I told him.

"That works for me." He said, extending his hand.

"It works for me too." I said, extending mine.

When Andrea and Mom came back in, they were hand and hand smiling. Andrea had done it again, she had won another one over with her charm. I could tell mom loved her already.

"Sean you have great taste. This one is a keeper. Don't let her go." Mom said, smiling, looking at me, then Michael.

"I don't plan on letting her go anywhere mom." I said, smiling, hugging Andrea around the waist.

On the drive home Andrea told me mom told her all about Michael. She said she was happy for me and hoped I would keep my word and get to know him. She said fathers were important and since I had one willing to be in my life, I should let him.

I placed my hand on her thigh as I drove over to the 405.

"She really is a keeper." I thought to myself.

CHAPTER SIX

Andrea

It had been several weeks since finding out Ty was for sure Andrew's. He came over to the Boutique to tell me about the drama he was having with Kelly's ol triflin ass. Andrew felt like he should approach his dealings with Kelly differently. He tried to talk to her about some type of custody arrangement, but she wouldn't agree to any terms. She was insistent that they try and work things out, but Andrew wasn't going for it.

"She said we should try and work it out, be a family because she never had one. I told that bitch she could go somewhere with all that noise." Andrew said, shaking his head.
"What did she say after you told her that?" Ashlynn asked, coming to sit on the counter near Andrew

"She just kept beggin'. Telling me how things would be different this time, and how I was the only dude she ever loved."

"That hoe sholl is full of sob stories!" Ashlynn said, rolling her eyes.

"You should have let me beat her ass a long time ago." I told him.

"I didn't want my sisters fighting my battles." Andrew said, smirking.

"No, what you said was, 'Nooooo, I don't want you to fight herrrrr, I loveee herrrrr'." I said mocking him.
Andrew laughed then said," I kind of wish I would have listened to the women in my life, You, Ash, Jamie and mom knew better than me. I couldn't see past the pussy and her trickin' on me to know the difference between love and anything else. I had never had a chick treat me like she did."

"Well if more men would think with their brain, and not their dicks the world would be a much better place." I said, high fiving Ashlynn.

"Whatever, you know that's not even my M.O. If I only thought with my dick, there would probably be a lot more nieces and nephews running around. You know, since chicks are always trying to get me to take my condom off, or trying to convince me that they are on the pill, and we don't need to use one." Andrew said, shaking his head at the thought.

"I hope you never fall for that bullshit." Ashlynn said, scrunching up her forehead, curling her upper lip.

"I never did, except once." Andrew said, placing his head in his hands.

"And 9 months later we end up with TY." I said, laughing.

"That's my dude though, so I wouldn't change a thing, except who his mama is." He said, laughing.

"So now what?" I asked.

"I don't know, She's being a dickhead about visitation and what not."

Andrew's phone rang, it was Kelly. He put her on speaker so we could hear the foolishness.

"Hello?"

"Hey babe, what you doing? she said, popping gum in his ear.

"I told you to stop calling me babe, and I'm kickin' it with my sisters, what do you want?"

"Oh yo sisters? Why you hangin' out with them broads for?"

"Don't disrespect my sisters, and I hope this call is about my son."

"Speaking of YO son, when you coming to see us?"

"I'm not ever coming to see y'all, but I will be by to pick up my son tomorrow."

"Dang you ain't gotta be all like that Drewski"

"I don't know why the fuck you keep coming up with these nicknames. We are not together, and I can assure you we never will be again."

"You must got you a new bitch huh? That's the only reason you wouldn't wanna come back home to mama."

"Nope, I don't have a new anything, but I wouldn't wanna come back to you because you're a lying, trifling, cheating ass hoe. Why would I want someone like that in my life?"

"I told you I would never cheat again."

"But you'd lie huh? I don't trust you. I did once upon a time, but you jacked that up. It's your fault we aren't together. I lost homies over you. Had my sisters mad at me and everything. So yea, I'm good on anything you think you could ever offer me again."

"I got your son though."

"I got my son too. It's on paper, clear as day that I'm his daddy."

"Well you can't see him unless I allow you. ."

"ALLOW?" Andrew said, raising his voice.

"Yea unless I allow you to. I control this shit, and you either do what I say, or you won't be seeing YO son!"

"Kelly you got life twisted. You don't control shit, and you sure as hell don't control me. I WILL see my son, and you can't stop me from doing that. I tried to go about this the easy way, but I see you leave me no other choice. I'm taking your ass to count!" Andrew said, hanging up on her, sweat forming on how brow.

"Chip calm down. I think court is the best thing you can do. Go file some custody papers. You've been paying child support since Ty was born. You do have rights. Go talk to a lawyer, and figure out your options." I insisted.

"Yea, and we got your back for sure. If you need me to go put hands on a bitch, I will." Ashlynn told him, hopping off the counter, acting like she was taking off her earrings.

"Calm down baby sis. She's not even worth breaking a nail over." He said, hugging Ashlynn.

Andrew hated for his sisters to fight, and Ashlynn has always been the scrappy one. If he gave her the word, she'd be all over Kelly.

"I'm gonna go make some calls. I'm done dealing with this bitch, and her antics." Andrew said, hugging me before he left.

Andrew was going to have a fight on his hands. I wished he had made a better choice than laying up with Kelly's ol ratchet behind. He was learning a very hard lesson, but I knew I would be there for him every step of the way. At the moment I was very grateful that I was with such a great man, and with no drama. That was the last thing I needed in my life.

Sean

It had been a few weeks since I met my dad. He had gone back to Texas, but we continued to get to know each other like he suggested. We talked on the phone a couple of times a week, and we really seemed to have a lot in common. He said he was thinking about moving back to California. He didn't have much family back in Texas, and he wanted to be closer to me and Mom. I knew mom would be all for that. After a few heart to hearts, it was clear she was still in love with him. He seemed like a good enough guy to me, but of course I still had some reservations. When I told Eli about meeting my dad, he was pumped for me. He told me that having a loving father in my life would be a great thing. He knew me well enough to know that I always wanted that for myself. I just had to make sure he knew I didn't play about my mama. If he thinks he's gonna come out here and use her in any way, then he's got another thing coming. Andrea told me to stop being so overprotective. She thought I was just trying to find reasons not to like him. Maybe she was right about that. I didn't completely trust him. How could I? I didn't know that man from Adam, and I was just supposed to trust him? Life just doesn't work like that. Andrea has never had to deal with anything like this. She's from a two parent family, and her parents are still happily married. Andrea's view will always be different from mine, but that was something I loved about her. Have I mentioned I love her? I mean, I'm IN LOVE with her. There had been a few times that Andrea has almost told me she loved me too, but she stops herself. I think she needs to know how I feel for sure, so I am planning something great for the two of us. Shelby is helping me out with it. She's bringing Justin with her so we can work out some details.

"Sean, come get these bags." Shelby said, handing me the diaper bag and her purse.

Justin was fast asleep in her arms.

"This boy feels like a sack of damn potatoes when he's asleep." Shelby said, struggling to get into my place.

"Here, let me take him."

"Thank you cuzzo, so how you doing?" She asked.

"I'm doing great. I have my baby boy here, and my favorite cousin in the whole world, what could be better?" I said smiling while I rocked Justin.

"Oh lord, yea, you're in love. You're being WAY too nice bruh." She said laughing.

"I'm not being too nice, don't act like you didn't know you were my favorite. But you're right, I am in love!" I sang.

"Uh huh." she said, shaking her head."So, what's the plan again? You gonna take her to dinner down in Redondo Beach, and then what?"

"Well I want to do dinner on the water, and then I have a hotel booked nearby."

"Ok do you need me to set up anything in the room while you're at dinner?"

"Yeah, I want you to get some purple roses, it's her favorite color. I need the petals to be sprinkled all over the room, and on the bed. Put your woman touch on it, and make it romantic."

"I got you. I think I'll spell I Love You out in the middle of the bed with them too."

"That would be great Shel! This is going to be perfect! And I'll also need for you to call her before the weekend, and make sure she's free to hang. I don't even want her to know I'm setting anything up, so ask her to come hang with you, have dinner or something."

Shelby stared at me with her head tilted, smiling."I think she's the one for you cuzzo. I've never seen you like this before, for anyone."

"No one was ever worth all of this. I think she's the one too. I almost want to get her a ring, but I don't know how she'd react to that."

"Why not?"

"Because we've been dating 8 months now and she still hasn't told me she loves me."

"well in her defense, it's been 8 months and you still haven't told her either."

"Touche'!"

"Yea, so quit playing. Don't let that girl get away."

"Oh, never! But I just want things to continue to progress naturally. I never want to rush anything."

"Ok, I'm gonna just follow your lead on this."

"Thanks for being supportive big head."

"Always chicken legs! Always."

"Whatever! my legs look damn good!" I said laughing, flexing my calves.

"I'm gonna have to tell Andrea to stop lying to you." shelby said laughing.

Since our business was done, we got comfortable on the sofa and caught up. I always loved spending time with Shelby. She understood me like no one else in the world, she's always only wanted the best for me.

I was a little sad when Shelby said she had to get home. I missed the days when she lived around the corner. Shelby came over for a purpose, and we were able to get all the plans laid out for the weekend. It was an evening my lady would ever forget.

CHAPTER SEVEN

Andrea

"Drea I'm so tired of getting here early! You know I don't get in until the sun comes up, and you got me here at 9 damn AM!"

The holidays were fast approaching which meant an increase in sales for the boutique. I had Ashlynn come in an hour earlier each day just so we could catch up with work.

"Do you like your job? I can give it to someone else if you'd like. All your damn complaining is getting old. If you weren't my baby sister I would definitely replace your whining ass." I snapped.

"I like my job just fine, and I appreciate you, you know that. But damn, cut a sista a break!" Ashlynn said, her brown eyes wide and sincere.

"It's nice to hear you say you appreciate me, but you work every last one of my nerves with your complaining. You gotta knock that shit off for real, or I might have to let you go." I said, my tone stern.

"Damn Drea, chill the fuck out a little bit. I'm just saying I'm tired, and it's early and. . ."

"And nothing," I said cutting her off "It's 9 a damn clock in the morning, that's not early by working peoples standards. I can bet you any other job you get won't pay you as well, and you'll have to get up much earlier, and stay much later for less pay. You didn't finish college, ain't much out there for you, and you won't get too far on your looks because your attitude sucks."

Ashlynn looked defeated. She got really quiet as she folded the shirts for the display table.

"You know I regret dropping out of school Drea, you don't have to throw it in my face." Ashlynn said quietly.

"I'm not throwing it in your face, I just need you to be realistic. You know I would prefer you to go back to school, then work here anyway. I just want you to be the best you can be, and sometimes I feel like I can only tell you what you want to hear, instead of the truth." I said looking her in the eyes.

"Well keep lying to me then Drea, because I don't like this snappy side of you at all." Ashlynn said smiling.

"I won't ever lie to you, but I will tone the snapping down. I have been in a mood all weekend." I confessed. Ashlynn deserved to be told off, but it was made worse by me feeling uneasy about my relationship with Sean.

"What's wrong, you on your period?"

"No I'm not on my period, It's Sean. He's been" I paused to search for the right word," different lately, and I don't know what's going on. We've been together almost 9 months now, and I think I know him pretty well by now, but things just feel, I don't know, off." I said sadly, trying to distract myself organizing receipts.

"I don't know Drea, you might just be trippin. He seems like a great dude to me. You're lucky you met him first because. ."

"Back up off my man you little hussy!" I laughed.

"I'm just sayin, if you don't want him slide him on over to mama and I'll do him right!" She said, shaking her little booty left and right.

Ashlynn always knew how to cheer me up. She is the type of girl who doesn't take life too seriously which is good, sometimes, but other times I wished she'd grow up.

When we were done working for the evening I decided I would call Sean. Since we've been dating I have never hid how I was feeling from him. Well maybe that's a lie. I was clearly in love with him and still hadn't told him yet, but I don't think that's bothering him. I need to tell him that things have been feeling different between us the last week or so. I need to know if I'm just tripping or if something really wrong.

Sean

I'd had quite the week finalizing all of the details for my weekend with Andrea. I had been so busy, I hadn't had much time to call her, and we usually talk every day. I was missing her like crazy, but things would make sense to her soon enough.

In the midst of all my planning, mom called me, and told me that she ran into Janae. She was a girl I used to crush on pretty bad from elementary through high school, but she never gave me the time of day romantically. We remained friends, mostly because I thought she was way out of my league. Mom told me that Janae had been looking for me for awhile, so she gave her my number. Imagine my shock, and surprise when Janae called me the other day.

"Sean!" Oh my Gah! I can't believe it's really you!" her voice bubbly and excited.

"Who is this?" I said, dryly. I was exhausted.

"Oh, so you're saying you don't recognize my voice? We used to be best friends!"

"This can't possibly be who I think it is?"

"Take a guess."

"Nae Nae?"

"Ugh! No one calls me that."

"Aww, it is you Nae Nae! What's up girl!?"

"Hey Sean! Not much is up. I've been looking for you for a couple of years now. I moved back out to california about 4 years ago."

"What have you been looking for me for? You're the one who fell off the face of the damn earth."

"I know, it's been one of my biggest regrets."

"Why'd you just drop me like that anyway?"

"It's a long story."

"I got time."

Janae explained to me how she had always had a crush on me, but didn't know how to say it. Little did she know, I felt the same way about her. She went on to tell me that when she went off to college at LSU, she thought about me every day. She told me that she dated a few guys, but she would always compare them to me, so things never really worked out. After college she was determined to tell me how she felt no matter the consequences, but she had a tough time locating me. She happened to run into my mom at the bank, and mom gave her my number.

"So. . . I don't know what else to say Sean. I've put it all out there."

"I don't know what to say either. I'm flattered that's for sure."

"Well I'm glad you're flattered." She said with a small laugh, trying to conceal her anxiety.

"I hope that didn't come off wrong. I mean, I always had the biggest crush on you. I just knew I wasn't your type back then, so I wasn't even going to try my luck. You knew how awkward I was with the ladies."

"Yea, I remember, and that was something I found so attractive. You were never trying to put on for anyone, you were just you. Most guys do too much, and it is a turn off."

"Well I didn't do enough, because I couldn't even tell you I liked you *like that* back then."

"Well you're telling me now, and I appreciate it. Shows me I wasn't the only one feeling the attraction."

"You weren't, that's for damn sure."

"Well listen Sean, maybe we can get together, and catch up in person?"

"Yes we can do that, it'll be good to see you. It's been a good 10 years."

"I know, don't remind me. How does tomorrow sound? I'll meet you wherever you want."

"Tomorrow it is. Let's meet at the pier. We can grab some food, and then maybe take a walk on the dock and catch up."

"Sounds perfect, I'll call you tomorrow."

"Okay Nae Nae!" I said teasing her

"You're getting punched as soon as I see you!"

"Yea, okay."

"Talk to you later." She said sweetly.

"You too."

I hung up the phone in a daze. The one person I crushed on throughout grade school was calling me, to tell me she was interested in me. I needed to make sure I looked good when I saw her. I've changed a lot since she last saw me. I bet she's still super fine too!

While I sat there thinking about Janae, I looked over, and saw the picture of me and Andrea resting on my nightstand. Her beautiful smile lighting up the entire frame. I was on the phone with Janae for about an hour, and I didn't think about Andrea once. I felt the guilt creep through my entire body. What was I thinking? I had committed to seeing Janae tomorrow.

"But, she is just a friend." I tried to rationalize with myself.

"Yea, but she's a friend I've had a crush on for years." I thought to myself, staring up at the ceiling. I thought my feelings for her were done and gone, now they are slowly coming back into focus. I love Andrea, but I need to see Janae, if nothing more than to close that chapter once and for all.

The next day after work I drove over to the pier. I told Janae to meet me at 3:45 at the mexican restaurant, so we could grab a quick bite. I was so nervous my palms were sweating and there was the biggest lump in my throat. I gave myself a pep talk before I got out of the truck.

She's just a girl. Don't be a weenie. You know how to talk to ladies now. Get it together dude. Show her what she missed out on. Channel Eli.

I got out of the truck, and walked inside of El Toritos. Janae was sitting inside waiting on me. She was still as beautiful as I remembered. Janae was tall, about 5'8" with the perfect coke bottle shape and dark brown beautiful skin. Her hair was braided in that style Janet Jackson's fine ass wore in Poetic Justice. She smiled when she saw me, with her beautiful teeth.(hey I have a thing for teeth, sue me) I swear I saw them glisten in the light. Her already tight eyes becoming even tighter when she smiled.

"Hey Handsome!" She said giving me a hug.

"Hey yourself." I said hugging her back.

Janae smelled so good, I could take in her scent the rest of the evening. Both of us holding on to each other like we never wanted to let go. After what seemed like a full minute of embracing, we let each other go. She looked at me up and down, noticing how much I've changed.

"You look good Sean, REAL good. The years have been nice to you." She said, smiling.

"You look good too, exactly as I remember you." I said, trying not to blush.

"Why thank you, I try and keep myself looking right." She said, flipping her braids off of her shoulder.

And look right she did. I never expected to see Janae again, and I surely never expected to feel like I was back in high school if we did run into each other.

The hostess walked us to a table, and I helped Janae into her seat. I couldn't help but check out her curves. Her body was right. I couldn't believe I was here with her. Janae McDaniels, the one woman I dreamed about marrying since I was 7.

Me and Janae sat and ate and talked for two hours. It seemed like no time had passed at all between us. She was still the same girl, and I was different, but in a good way. I had confidence,and swag and wasn't afraid to speak my mind like I used to be. Being ugly can do that to a brotha, but times had changed. As we stood getting up to leave, Janae grabbed my hand interlocking her fingers with mine. It caught me by surprise, but for some reason, I didn't pull away. She smiled, and winked at me as we headed for the door. I guess she hadn't noticed the stunned look on my face. Before we could make it outside Ashlynn walked in with two of her friends. When she saw me, she smiled, then looks over at Janae, then down at our interlocked hands. Ashlynn went from smiling to scowling, twisting her lips to the side of her face.

"Hey Sean." She said, scrunching up her nose like she smelled something rotten. I watched as her brown face turning red. I didn't know that was even possible.

"Hey Ashlynn. What you doing here?" I asked nonchalantly.

"Oh, I'm here with my girls for happy hour, what are YOU doing here?" She says as she motions to my hand holding with Janae.

"Oh I was just out with a friend from school." I said, quickly letting go of Janae's hand. I suddenly felt like I was trapped in a cage.

"Oh a friend huh? I was just with Andrea, She must have not known about your *friend*." Ashlynn said sarcastically.

"No she doesn't. I haven't talked to her much this week. It was kind of spur of the moment. My mom. . "I said, feeling like my explanation was pointless. I could feel Janae staring at me.

Ashlynn pushed past me to Janae.

"Hi, I'm Ashlynn, Sean's GIRLFRIENDS sister." She said, extending her hand to Janae.

"Hi, I'm Janae, I'm. . . hell. . . I guess I'm nobody." her eyes falling to her feet. Janae said, as she stormed out.

"Janae! Wait!" I called after her.

"You betta leave that hoe alone! And you better believe I'm about to tell Andrea all about this. And to think I was just telling my sister I thought you were a great guy." Ashlynn said glaring at me.

I didn't say a word as I ran out after Janae. She was standing by her car with tears in her eyes. I didn't know what to say. Everything happened so fast I didn't have time to gather myself. I walked over to her, thinking very carefully before I spoke. Call it a hunch, but I knew this wouldn't end well.

"Janae, I'm so sorry about that." I told her, reaching for her hand.
Janae looked at me with tears ready to fall from her lower lashes. Suddenly, a frown formed on her face. Before I knew it, Janae had slapped me hard in the face. The pain shot straight to the back of my head as I stumbled backward holding my eye.

"Sorry about what!? HUH!? What the fuck are you sorry for Sean!? The fact that you didn't tell me you have a girlfriend?" she spat, taking a few steps toward me, her fists balled up. I was reeling from the pain of her hand making contact with my face.

"Damn I guess I deserved that." I said, finally removing my hand from my eye. I could already feel it swelling. "I was gonna say I was sorry for Ashlynn being so rude."

"She wasn't being rude! She was just looking out for her sister. I would have done the same thing. Hell I would have embarrassed your ass if I were her. Why didn't you mention you had a girlfriend?" she said, angry veins popping up in her neck when she spoke.

"You didn't ask me. I mean, it didn't come up, and honestly I hadn't thought about her today while I was with you. I was all too consumed with seeing you again I hadn't even thought. . . I didn't think." I admitted feeling guilty.

"So what are you saying?" She asked.

"I'm saying I'm sorry if I hurt your feelings. I do have a girlfriend, and I love her. I would never do anything to hurt her." I said looking her in the eyes.

"Then why are you here with me?" she asked plainly.

"I needed some closure I guess. I knew I had changed, and I guess I just wanted you to see that."

"Well that's real fucking mature Sean. This was all just a waste of my fucking time. I thought it was the start of something new. You let me play myself. I should slap your ass again." She said, her brow dipping down further toward her nose as she opened and closed her hands. I took a step away from her. I wasn't sure if she would follow through with her threat, and I wasn't trying to find out, although I probably deserved it.

"I didn't intend for any of this to happen. I care about you and I always have. If I wasn't in a relationship I would see where things go with you, but our time has passed. I'm sorry Janae."

"How serious is this relationship with your girlfriend?" the anger disappeared from her face once again replaced by sadness.

"Pretty serious. I was thinking of asking her to be my wife this weekend." I said, looking away.

Janae looked up at me with tears in her eyes.

"I'm sorry. I don't know what made me think you'd just be here, single, waiting on my return. I blew it years ago when I didn't tell you how I felt. I'll probably regret it forever. Your girlfriend is a lucky woman."

"Janae you never even let on that you liked me. I know you had to be aware that I was crushing on you big time. But really, I'm the lucky one. Andrea means the world to me, and I could just have ruined it. I know her sister is going to make it seem like we were in the middle of the restaurant fucking." I said shaking my head.

"Well look, if you need me to talk to her, I will do that for you, you know, since I slapped you in your face and all." she said sincerely.

"Thanks Janae, and again I'm sorry. I never wanted to hurt you. That's just not the type of man I am. I really don't know what came over me." I said, hugging her. I really hated hurting her feelings. I also hated that I'd have a shiner tomorrow.

"Bye Sean." she said, releasing herself from my embrace.

Janae got in her car, and drove away. I took a walk up the pier to think. I knew I would be in trouble with Andrea. I just had to hope It didn't mean the end for us.

CHAPTER EIGHT

Andrea

"You saw him doing what with who!?" I said loudly into the phone.

Apparently Ashlynn was out with her friends, and bumped into Sean. She was so worked up with every word she spoke, my only reaction was to get worked up too. I was getting angrier by the second.

"I saw yo nigga up here at the pier with some broad!" She repeated.

"And did you talk to him?"

"Yep I got in his shit about being up there holding hands with the bitch. L.A ain't that damn big to be doing dirt! I knew that nigga was too good too to be true!"

It was hard for me to wrap my mind around what she was telling me. I knew things felt a little off between us, but I didn't think he was cheating on me.

"I can't believe this! He's been seeing someone else, that's why things have been weird between us. I can't believe this shit!" I screamed. My entire body became so hot, I had to remove my sweater.

"Drea calm down. You want me to come get you so we can beat his ass? You know I'm always down."

"No, enjoy your meal. I'm gonna get to the bottom of this." I said, fanning myself trying to calm down.

"You sure? I don't want you doing nothing crazy by yourself. Let ME be the crazy one." I could just imagine Ashlynn pacing back and forth, eyes all bucked out and crazed.

"I'm not going to do anything crazy, but I am also not gonna be played for a fool. Mark did enough of that when I was with him." I said, shaking my head, mad at myself for comparing Sean and Mark.

"Well let me call Andrew and have him handle it for you." She insisted.

"No, Andrew has his own drama going on right now. I don't want to involve him in any of mine." I knew Andrew would shake the shit out of Sean if he ever thought he was doing me wrong. I needed to make sure he stayed all the way out of this mess.

"Ok Drea, but if you need me for anything I'm here. If I don't hear from you again tonight I'll see you at work in the morning."

"Thanks sis, I love you."

"I love you too!"

No sooner than I hang up the phone with Ashlynn my phone started ringing again. I didn't want to talk to anyone. I was too angry and needed to get my thoughts together before my head exploded.

"Hello!" I said aggressively.

"Uh. . . hey Andrea, it's Shelby."

"Oh hey Shelby." I said trying to sound more pleasant.

"Did I catch you at a bad time?"

"No it's cool. What's up girl?" I asked. If anyone knew Sean was seeing someone else it would be Shelby. She was the one person in this world that he shared everything with besides , you know, Eli and I knew he wouldn't spill those type of beans, not even on his deathbed.

"Oh, I was just calling to see if Sean told you I wanted us to hang out on saturday. There's a nice little restaurant next to the Hilton near the beach."

"No he hasn't told me anything. I actually haven't spoken to him much this week." I told her, annoyance sprinkled through my words.

"Maybe I spoke too soon. He was supposed to have already called and made sure you were free."

"Oh well maybe you just beat him to it."

"Ok girl. I'm sorry, but do you think you'll be able to make it?"

"I think I'm free."

"Ok, it's a date." I said, rolling my eyes.

"See you then!" Shelby said cheerfully as she hung up.

I had my own plans for my evening with Shelby. I was going to find out if she knew anything about who or what Sean had been doing lately. I had a feeling she knew, and girlfriend to girlfriend I just hoped she would be honest with me.

Sean

"Sean!" Shelby said.

"What's up Shel?" I said, sounding defeated. I had walked down the pier and stopped when I found a bench. I was sitting there trying to figure out what to do when Shelly called me.

"I just called Andrea, and she's free Saturday!" She said, almost unable to contain herself.

"I don't even know if that's still on."

"Uh oh, what the hell happened?"

"I think I may have fucked everything up." I said, placing my face in my palms.

"Cuzzo, what's wrong? You've been planning this for over a month. You got me all involved, and when I do my part I look like a damn fool!" She scolded.

"I know, I know. It was something I premeditated. It's just that Janae hit me up and. . ."

"Janae McDaniels? The one you had the biggest crush on forever?"

"Yep, the very one." I said, slumping over on the bench.

"What does she have to do with anything?"

"Well she kinda called me Thursday, and we talked on the phone for a while, and tonight I met up with her for dinner, and. . "

"Wait, so instead of telling your woman you had a surprise for her, and to meet you at the hotel this weekend you were out with another woman? Do you know how bad that sounds dude?"

"I know it sounds bad, but you know how I felt about Janae. When she called I couldn't think about anything but seeing her again. I really wanted to show her how much I changed. You know, show her what she missed out on."

"That's fucked up man. She kind of did you wrong by not talking to you anymore when she went away to college, but when she calls, you just run back to her. What kind of shit is that!? You better hope Andrea doesn't find out about it."

"If she doesn't already know, she will soon. Her sister Ashlynn saw us there, and Janae was holding my hand and. . ."

"You got caught holding hands with a chick? Lord! I don't know man, you may not be able to get out of this one. You say it was innocent, but I bet it didn't look that way. Use your fucking head! You're gonna lose a good thing because you're being so stupid." She said, disgust in her voice.

"Yea, Janae wasn't too pleased either. She smacked me so hard, my left eye is a little swollen."

"Good, you deserved it for playing games."

"I know I did. I just don't know what to do now. I don't know if I should call Andrea, and talk to her about it or what." I said, leaning back looking up into the sky.

"Well you better do something quick, because if she thinks you were stepping out on her, this could all be over." She assured me.

I knew Shelby was right. I knew I had fucked up. I knew I could lose Andrea, and that was the last thing I ever wanted to happen. I just wanted Janae to see what she had missed out on, which I'm now realizing was a bad move on my part. I could potentially lose the love of my life.

"I'm gonna go see her. I think talking to her face to face would be best." I said, heading in the direction of my truck.

"Well go do it now. Good luck. Call me and let me know how it goes." She said, concern in her words.

"Thanks, I'll call you. Love you Shel."

"Love you too."

Andrea

After I hung up with Shelby I was fuming! I didn't know whether to call Sean now and cuss his ass out, or if I should play it cool until I was face to face with Shelby. What I did know was that I didn't want to be played for a fool every again by anyone. I had been there and done that and could probably write a book about it. Sean was the last person I ever expected to betray me.

I paced my living room, playing out the events of the past week in my head. As close as Sean and I had become, as much time as we spent with each other, I don't know when he'd even have time to start up another relationship. When would he even have the time to keep two going at the same time? The other women sure was getting the short end of the stick if that were the case.

My phone rang again, the number on the caller ID was one I didn't recognize. I hesitantly answered it, something just told me I should.

"Hello ma'am, do you know an Andrew LaSalle?" A woman's voice asked.

"Yes, He's my brother, how can I help you?"

"I'm sorry to tell you this over the phone, but he's been hurt pretty badly. I'm the ER nurse over at Kaiser on Cadillac, and we found his phone in his pocket. We tried a few numbers, but you were the only one who answered."

"Oh my God! Oh my GOD!" I screamed.

"Calm down ma'am. We are doing everything we can for him. If you can please make your way down here. Maybe you'll be able to help with a few questions."

"I'm on my way!" I said as I hung up.

I didn't know what was going on, but I knew my night couldn't get much worse. I grabbed my purse and keys, and headed out the front door. I opened it to find Sean on my porch.

CHAPTER NINE

Sean

I got to Andrea's house as she was rushing out the door.

"Andrea can I talk to you?" I asked, following her to her car.

"Not right now! I have to get to the hospital!" She snapped, tears in her eyes.

"What's wrong? Did something happen!?"

"Andrew is in the hospital. I don't know what's wrong, I just have to get there."

"I'm coming with you." I insisted.

Andrea unlocked her car, and didn't put up a fuss when I hopped in. She started the car, and headed up LaCienega. We sat in silence, her watching the road with tears running down her face, and me staring at her. I wanted to comfort her, but at that moment, I just didn't know how. Knowing how Ashlynn operates, I knew she called Andrea before I walked out the door. I was 100% sure Andrea knew about my meeting up with Janae, but at this moment that didn't matter.

We made it to the hospital, and I followed her quietly as we made our way through the doors of the ER.

"I'm here for Andrew LaSalle." Andrea told the man at the triage station.

He made a phone call, and told Andrea to go to room 4. We headed through the double doors, and found the room. There was a nurse in the room, and she explained to Andrea that Andrew had been beaten up pretty badly. His jaw was broken, and he had a few broken ribs and a broken leg. Both of his eyes were swollen nearly shut, and he had been sedated to keep him relaxed.

"Who did this to my brother?" Andrea asked frantically.

"We don't know ma'am. Some people found him near an alley a few miles from here. They called 911. The paramedics found his wallet, and phone on him. Once they brought him here I started making calls." The nurse told Andrea

"Is that all the information you have?" Andrea asked.

"That's all I have ma'am. The police have been by here to ask him questions, but he couldn't stay conscious long enough to answer them. They asked us to give them a call once he was up and alert."

"Thank you." Andrea said, as more tears fell from her eyes.

The nurse walked out, and left us with Andrew. The brotha had gotten it bad. Andrea could hardly look at him. She buried her head into my chest, and sobbed loudly. I wrapped my arms around her and let her cry. It hurt like hell to see her so upset. It hurt even worse that the person she was hurting for was someone she was so close to.

"Who the fuck would do this to my brother!" Andrea said angrily just above a whisper. "They didn't take his wallet or his phone so he wasn't robbed. This shit had to be personal! Who would do this!?"

"I don't know babe. This is really messed up. What do you need me to do? Anything?" I said into her hair, her head still on my chest.

"Take my phone and call Ashlynn. Tell her what happened, and have her call my parents. I can't . . .I can't do it. I'll break all the way down." She said, handing me her phone.

Ashlynn was probably the last person on earth who wanted to hear from me, but this was important. I had to suck it up and call her. I know how important family is to all of them.

"Hey Drea, what's up? You call that trifling nigga?" Ashlynn said, as she answered the phone.

"Ashlynn, this is Sean, Andrea told me to call you." I said nervously. The last thing I wanted was for her to go off on me, not right now.

"What the hell are you doing calling me? And why you got my sister's phone?" She said, raising her voice.

"Ashlynn I didn't call you to fight. Me and Andrea are at the hospital. Andrew is hurt. He got beat up pretty bad. He's not in good shape. Andrea wants you to call your parents." I explained.

"Oh my God! Are you being serious right now?" She yelled.

"I am. We are at Kaiser with him now. He's knocked out, but they said he'll be okay."

Ashlynn started to cry, and all I wanted to do was comfort her too. It had been a long night for everyone. We just needed to be there for Andrew.

"Okay, okay, let me call Mama and Daddy, and we'll come up there. I can't believe this.``she said, weeping.

"It'll be ok Ashlynn. We'll see you when you get here." I said, hanging up the phone.

I still wanted to talk to Andrea about tonight. I want her to know it wasn't what it looked like. That I didn't tonight, nor have I ever cheated on her, and I never would. I let my pride overrule, and felt like I had something to prove to Janae. All that got me was a slap in the face. I don't know how Andrea would take that, but she had to hear it from me.

I walked back into the room to find Andrea in a chair next to her brother. She laid her head as close to him as she could without touching him. I figured she thought she might hurt him if she got too close. I could hear her saying something to him. I stepped in a little closer to get a listen. She wasn't talking to him, she was praying over him.

Lord please heal my brothers body, his spirit and his soul. I ask that you bring him though this just the way he was before. I know he hasn't always been the best person Lord but his heart has always been in the right place. Lord I ask you wrap your healing arms around my Andrew. He is my best friend Lord and for selfish reasons, I need to keep him around. I ask this in your name Lord Amen.

Sean

We had been at the hospital for about 45 minutes. By that time Andrea had calmed down. She told me before her family showed up, that she has always been the strong one, and tonight was no exception. She had excused herself to the restroom to straighten her face. While she was gone Shelby called me. I'm sure she was trying to figure out what was happening, since it had been hours since we last spoke. The phone rang 4 times before I answered.

"Cuz, is everything okay?" Shelby asked in a panicked tone.

"Yea, calm down. I'm at the hospital with Andrea right now."

"Wait, what!? Is she okay?"

"She's fine. Her brother Andrew was beaten up, and he was brought to the ER."

"Oh that's horrible."

"I know, so I'm just here with her for whatever she needs."

"That's good. I'm glad you're there, but did you guys get a chance to talk about earlier?"

"No I never got the chance. As soon as I got to her house she was on her way out of the door. I just hopped in her car, and went with her. I don't think the time is right to bring it up. Not right now."

"I agree. Well I hope everything is okay with her brother. I just want everything to be okay between the two of you." Shelby said sounding sad.

"Me too Shel. Let me get off this phone though. I love you and I'll call you tomorrow." I told her

"Love you too Sean."

I waited with Andrea for her family to show up, they came within an hour of me hanging up with Ashlynn. Mr and Mrs. LaSalle walked in and hugged Andrea, then me. Ashlynn walked past me straight to Andrea, and cried into her shoulder. They all stared at me, but no one asked what happened to my face, I was grateful. The next few hours seemed to drag on forever, and I felt very helpless in the situation. We were in the waiting area because the doctor needed to examine Andrew. Andrea sat and filled her family in on what we knew. Mrs. LaSalle was visibly shaken up, while Mr. LaSalle grew increasingly angry. It seemed that everyone had the same idea of who the suspect was that had set evenings events in motion: Kelly, Andrew's baby mama.

"That bitch probably set him up daddy!" Ashlynn said in between sobs.

"I'm having that same thought baby girl." Mr. LaSalle said.

"I was thinking that too, but I have been trying to remain positive." Andrea said.

"I don't even want to think about that. I don't like that child, but I don't want to think she'd ever hurt my baby. And Phil, don't plant those ideas in the girls heads." Mrs. LaSalle said.

"Mama you know you are thinking the same thing. I hope it's not the case, but who else would be that upset with him." Andrea said.

"I know baby. Let's just pray she had nothing to do with it. Let's just pray it was random." Mrs. LaSalle said, laying her head on her husband's shoulder. He stroked her hair in an effort to comfort her.

I sat there silent. From all the stories Andrea has told me about Kelly, and the one time I saw her in action, they all had a point. She seemed very capable of setting him up for the beat down. A woman scorned was nothing to mess with. The few fellas I hang with have all had at least one. They always made me glad I didn't play the type of games with women the way they did. That is, until tonight. I still wanted to talk to Andrea, explain to her I have been faithful and committed but tonight probably won't be the night.

The Doctor came into the waiting room. He told us that Andrew would be fine. Once his broken bones were healed there would be no permanent damage. That was a relief to us all. The doctor said that Andrew was starting to wake up, and was asking for Andrea. He informed us that once he was moved to a room upstairs, we could all go up and see him. He told Andrea she could come back with him. She stood and started to follow the Doctor. Then, she turned around slowly like she was forgetting something, and came and grabbed my hand so I could go with her.

Andrea

I grabbed Sean's hand, and made him come with me to see Andrew. At that moment I needed him. The doctor led us into Andrew's room. He heard the curtain move, and he called my name weakly.

> "Chip." I said, trying to hold back tears. "I'm here."
>
> "Drea, they fucked me up." He said, trying to touch his swollen face.
>
> "Who did Chip? Who did this to you."
>
> "I don't know them niggas."
>
> "How many were there?"
>
> "Two, I think." he said, weakly.
>
> "They just came and started fighting you?"

"No, they asked did I know Kelly, and was my name Drew."

"Fuck! I knew Kelly had something to do with this shit! I'm going to kill that bitch!" I said, raising my voice.

"Calm down Sis. You making my head hurt worse." He said, trying to smile.

"I'm sorry Chip. Me, Daddy and Ash all thought she might be behind this. You don't have any other enemies."

"I know. She's bitter."

"Bitter don't lead to all of this."

"I guess for her it does." he said, trying to keep the slits of his eyes open.

"Chip, I need you to get some rest. I need you to heal all the way okay. I love you so much. I've been sitting around here praying like crazy."

"I know, I heard you." He said squeezing my hand.

Andrew and I have a bond like no other. He was my first friend even though we are a few years apart. He's always been my shoulder to lean on. I've always been closer to him than any friends I've ever had. Ashlynn even gets jealous of how close we are. Once he confirmed Kelly had something to do with this, all I could see was red. I wanted to kill that girl. Beat her the way she had my brother beaten. I was snapped out of those thoughts when Sean touched my shoulder.

"Andrea." He said softly.

I turned to look at him.

"Andrew drifted back off to sleep. Maybe we should let him rest." He said.

I kissed Andrew on the forehead and quietly left the room. Sean could tell something more than seeing my brother like that was wrong with me. Before he could ask I confessed.

"Kelly! That bitch really did set my brother up! The cops better get her before we do!"

"Remember the nurse said the cops would be back, maybe we should tell them what Andrew said." Sean Suggested.

"Maybe, or maybe I should grab Ash and we go to pay her a visit!"

"Don't do that. It could only make matters worse." He said.

I felt the fire inside of me getting bigger. I was infuriated that Kelly had set my brother up, and suddenly I remembered I was upset with Sean too. I snapped!

"You got your fucking nerve Sean! Don't think I don't know about you seeing some other bitch! Don't think I don't know that you've been stepping out on me." I said, raising my voice, as I backed him into a corner.

"I wanted to explain that to you, that's why I came. . ."

"That's why you what!? I would say you better have a good fucking excuse for things, but at this point I really don't give two shits! And what happened to your fucking face?" I said stepping into his personal space.

"Andrea, please hear me out." He said, his eyes starting to water.

"Go head, give me your bullshit story." I said, glaring at him..

Sean told me that Janae was someone from his past, someone who hadn't given him the time of day back then. He said when she confessed her feelings for him he just wanted to show her what she had missed out on, since she stopped talking to him once she went to college. He confessed he got carried away by agreeing to go to dinner with her, and when she grabbed his hand, he didn't notice until Ashlynn walked in.

"Then when I went outside to find her, she slapped me, hard." he said, patting the swelling.

"So you got caught up in your lies by Ash and ol' girl."

"If I thought I had been caught, don't you think I would have acted more suspicious?

Don't you think I would have stayed and begged Ashlynn not to call you? I didn't think until after the fact that you probably wouldn't be pleased with me hanging out with another woman, but I promise you baby, nothing went on. I love you Andrea. I would never do anything to hurt you. You are the best thing that has ever happened to me." He said with tears running down his face. "That's the problem Sean, you weren't thinking about me. I can't mean that much to you if I don't even cross your mind. Ashlynn told me that woman didn't even know you had a girlfriend, why would that type of information be withheld?" I asked, folding my arms across my chest.

"I wasn't. . . I didn't. . . I'm sorry." He said, lowering his head.

"I'm sorry too." I said, as I walked into the waiting room to be with my family leaving him standing there.

Andrea

Yesterday all seemed like a blur. I woke up curled up in a chair in a hospital room, my parents and sister on the other side of the room all piled onto the sofa. I don't even remember falling asleep. After I had it out with Sean, I went and told my parents what Andrew said about Kelly. We were all upset and trying to figure out how to handle it. By 11pm Andrew was moved to his room, and we all went up there and settled in. We knew we weren't going home that night. Andrew was in and out of consciousness with the pain meds they gave him to keep him comfortable. As my family slept, I had a million thoughts racing through my mind. In the forefront was making sure Kelly got what was coming to her, one way or another. Then, my thoughts would drift to Sean. I know the things that I said to him were harsh, but he deserved every word. I didn't know whether or not I could be with a man who doesn't even think it's important to tell people he has a woman. I couldn't understand where he was coming from, and I was too pissed off to listen to his explanation. I just knew I couldn't go another second with him thinking I would just let it slide. He was lucky that ol' girl slapped him before I could get my hands on him. I would have to deal with that later. I needed to focus on my brother.

I got up from the chair and went over to the bed Andrew was resting in. I looked at his face all battered, swollen and bruised. I looked at his leg they had propped up and in a cast. I watched him sleep as peaceful as he could given the circumstances. A shift nurse had just walked in to check on my brother. I smiled at her politely, grabbed my phone from the chair, and excused myself. Kelly was going to hear from me.

I dialed her number not expecting her to answer. she picked up on the second ring.

"Hello." Kelly said in her husky morning voice.

"Kelly, I know what you did." I said, a growl in my tone.

"What!? Who the hell is this? It's too early for people to be playing on my phone."

"This is Andrea, and I know what you did to my brother."

"Bitch please, I didn't do anything to your damn brother!"

"Trick do you know he's in the hospital right now? Do you know he has broken bones, and a swollen face. Did your minions tell you what they did to him?" I said, tasting the fire in every question.

"They didn. . . I mean I don't know what you're talking about."

"Oh you know what I'm talking about and you're gonna get yours hoe! Mark my words!"

"I'm not getting shit! My hands are clean. Your brother must have messed with the wrong muthafuckas. If he got his ass kicked, he probably deserved it."

"And you're gonna deserve everything that's coming your way, believe me."

"Yea okay Andrea. Are you done now? I'm gonna go back to sleep, because you woke me up for some bullshit I don't even care about. Andrew ain't dead, you should be happy I told them niggas to go easy." She said, then got silent, realizing she had just confessed..

"Oh, you know you done fucked up now right? You admitted it you dumb bitch. If you think I haven't been recording this conversation, you're as dumb as you look." I laughed.
Kelly was silent for a moment, then she said, "I don't care if you were recording. What's that supposed to mean?"

"It means you should be expecting the cops very soon." I said, hanging up in her face.

I had used Andrew's phone to record the conversation. I knew she was dumb enough to admit her part. As much as I wanted to beat the dog shit out of her myself, I didn't want to cause more trouble. The police said they would be back here today. When I present them with this evidence, that hoe will be going to jail.

When I walked back into the room everyone was staring at me. I guess my end of the conversation was a little loud.

"What happened?" Ashlynn asked, rubbing her eyes.
"Kelly just caught herself up." I said holding up Andrew's phone.
"She said she did this?" Andrew asked.
"She did, and as soon as the cops come back I'll let them hear what she said." I told him.
"I filed those papers." Andrew said.
"The custody papers?" Mom asked.
"Yea." Andrew said, trying to focus his eyes.
"You couldn't have done that at a better time son, maybe that's what made her so upset." Dad said.

"I think it was. If she's willing to hurt me to keep me away from him then it backfired on that ass. Any court would give me my son now." Drew said, trying to smile.

"Ty belongs with you anyway, with us." I said, taking a seat next to Andrew's bed.

"He doesn't need to be with that wack ass hoe." Ashlynn said.

Mom shot her a look of disapproval. Ashlynn knew mom was no saint, but she sure didn't like any of us cussing around her.

Ashlynn said, "Sorry Ma, but that bitch will get what's coming to her. Look what she did to my brother. The cops better get here quick."

Ashlynn may have been a petite caramel skinned beauty, but she was scrappy. She used to fight so much in school because the girls were always jealous of her. It wasn't her fault their boyfriends were always sniffing around. She always had to defend herself, she had no other choice. It probably wasn't the best idea for daddy to put her in boxing classes when she was 10. He saw that she was being bullied, and wanted her to be able to defend herself if she needed to. That's partly why Andrew never let her loose on Kelly, It wouldn't have been pretty.

About an hour later, the police showed up. I played the recording for them, and they told me that was all they needed to go arrest her. Andrew provided her address, and the address of her mother just in case she thought she could hide out there. The police left, on a mission to find Kelly. I was relieved that they were going to arrest that hoe. I had been awake for hours, and was exhausted. I made sure Andrew was alright with me going home to shower, and to grab some food. Mom and dad said they would stay with him.

I pulled up in my driveway, and thanked God for this outcome. My brother would be fine, and the person who got him hurt would be locked up, my day was looking up. I wrapped my arms around the steering wheel, and laid my head on it for a few moments. I was drained both physically and emotionally, I just wanted to curl up in my bed and catch a nap for a few hours. I knew I wouldn't be able to sleep though, I wanted to get back to the hospital and be with

Andrew.

My eyes were closed when I heard a loud knock on my driver side window. I snapped out of my trance to find Mark's dumb ass face smiling at me. I rolled my eyes so hard, I almost lost them in the back of my head. What the hell could he even want? I had nothing to say to him. And furthermore, how did he know where I lived? I opened the door and stepped out.

I flipped my curls from my face,"First, how do you know where I live and second, what the fuck do you want?"

"Calm down Andrea." He said, flashing the smile I once adored." I stopped by your store as you were leaving the other day because I wanted to talk to you. I followed you home, but kept driving. I figured I'd pop up on you another day."

"And you thought that was a good idea I'm guessing? That's called stalking Mark, and I don't take kindly to it." I said, glaring at him, wiping the smile off his face.

"I don't consider it stalking. We shared something special, and I know we can get it back." He said with pleading eyes.

"You have GOT to be shitting me! You had a whole other life, in a whole other state! You are a liar! You are a cheater! You are a loser! I wouldn't EVER consider being anything to you again. If you were on fire, I wouldn't even let a stranger piss on your dumb ass." I said, my finger in his face.

"Andrea, come on. You were with that chump at the chicken place, I know I can treat you better than him. I've changed. I'm not that same guy that did those things to you."

"Really? How's your fiance? Your child?" I said, pursing my lips together. Having him in my personal space was making me feel sick. After the evening I had, today wasn't the day for any extra bullshit.

Mark looked dumbstruck as his eyes fell to his feet."Uh, my child is fine. He's back in Texas with his mother and we're not together anymore."

"That's great! Now what does any of this have to do with me? She got smart on your ass and finally left, and you think it's a good idea to crawl your ass back to me? Mark, you can't be THAT stupid. You know I'm with someone and you KNOW I can't stand your ass. Get out of my driveway and go on with your life. Go scam some other chick, because I will never be the one again." I said slamming my car door. "Don't make me call the police."
I walked into my house putting the locks on the door after I closed it.. If Mark was crazy enough to follow me home, I wouldn't put breaking into my house past him. I didn't trust him, and I didn't feel safe. My house phone rang as I turned the final lock. I rushed to grab it before whoever was on the other end hung up.

CHAPTER TEN

Sean

"Andrea, please don't hang up." I pleaded.

"Just what the fuck I needed! Can a sista catch a break today! Damn!"

"I just wanted to talk to you, I need to talk to you."

"First Mark stalks me, and shows up at my place, then the man I thought I could trust comes calling me. I don't know if I want to hear what you have to say." I told him.

"Mark!? Wait, what? Do you need me to come over there?"

"I don't need you to do anything Sean, I can take care of myself"

"I just. . . nevermind." I said.

I didn't want to fight with her. After she cussed me out that the hospital I caught a cab home. I felt like shit for hurting her and I needed to make it right.

"Andrea please, just give me 5 minutes of your time." I begged.

I didn't have time to worry about Mark, he blew his chance with her years ago. I was just praying I hadn't blown mine.

Andrea allowed me to say what I needed to say. I told her how sorry I was about everything. I confessed that although I had grown up, some parts of me were still insecure.

"I have been in love with you since our first exchange at Ralphs. I have told anyone who would listen, that I knew you were the one I was going to spend the rest of my life with." I couldn't control the tears from flowing as I poured my heart out to her. I had nothing to lose, but Andrea.

After I was done talking Andrea said," Are you done?"

"I could go on forever really babe. My love for you runs deep. I can't sleep, eat, even breathe without you." I said sincerely.

"Sean, you hurt me, and that is something I never thought I would say about you. I'm not saying I never want to be with you again, but you have to give me some time and space to think about things. I don't want to be played for a fool. I was JUST reminded how big of a fool I have been with Mark showing up here."

"Y'all broke up before you moved into that place. How did he know where you live?" I asked, concerned.

"He said he followed me home."

"So he's stalking you? Do you need me to come. . ."

"No."Andrea said cutting me off. "I don't need you to come over here. I can handle it. Just give me some time and space like I said. I have to think about this. Andrew is laid up in that hospital, and I don't need this right now. I really don't. I'll be in touch Sean." She said, then she hung up.

I was left sitting there with my phone in my hand stuck. I almost wanted to call her back, but she wanted space, and I was going to give her that. I loved that woman and I would wait a million years if I had to. I needed to clear my head. I grabbed my keys, and headed out the door.

I thought about places I could go, and I needed someone to talk to. Someone who would actually listen to what I had to say. Shelby was annoyed with me, and I hadn't told Mom how I screwed up andI wouldn't hear the end of it. I drove up Manchester until I ended up at the beach. I parked my car and walked until there was nowhere else to go. I stood on those rocks and looked out into the choppy water. I knew nothing would ever be the same with Andrea, but I could only hope we could move forward. I decided I needed a man to talk to. Eli wouldn't be of any help. He'd just tell me Andrea was overreacting, and I knew that wasn't the case. He didn't have the same respect for women as I did. His mom walked out on him and his dad when he was 7, that's why women were just objects to him. I knew Andrea had a good reason to be upset, and I didn't want to hear him telling me otherwise. I took my phone out my pocket and dialed the only Texas number in the phone book. I needed to talk to my dad.

"Son!" He said, happy to hear see my number pop up.

"Hey Mike. . I mean Dad. That still sounds weird to say." I said.

"I know, it'll take some time. Don't force it." He said, chuckling.

"Yeah. . ."I said, unable to find any words.

"Sean, everything okay? You're not sounding like yourself."

"No Dad, everything is all bad actually. I think I may have screwed up my situation with Andrea." I confessed.

"You didn't step out on her did you?" He asked, sounding concerned.

"No. . Well.. . . Kinda." I said, eyes watering again.

"Tell me what happened Sean. I'm here for you." He said, and I believed him. I trusted him. I knew he would lead me in the right direction to fix what was broken.

I told him everything. About how I grew up awkward. I told him about Janae, and how she just dissed me when we left for college. I told him about the date, and how Andrea found out about it. I told him I loved her more than anything, almost as much as I loved my momma, so he knew that was serious business. I started to sob when I told him that I didn't think I could fix it.

"Sean, son, You can fix it. It's not beyond repair." He said with sincerity.

"But how? How can I get her to understand, to believe that nothing like this will ever happen again?" I asked.

"She feels hurt and betrayed. It's obvious she's been hurt before. You made her wall go up. You need to break that wall back down. You said you guys hadn't said I love you yet, and now you've told her a number of times. Right now she doesn't hear it. I can bet you she hasn't even heard you when you've said it. I suggest you show her you love her. Actions speak much louder than words." He said, really sounding like a dad, my dad.

I thanked him, and told him how much I appreciated him and his advice. I knew what I needed to do. Something that would either have her forgive me, or she would simply walk away if her heart told her so.

Andrea

had called Shelby to tell her I wouldn't be meeting up with her on Saturday. I know she meant well, but I just couldn't sit there with her and be fake, especially knowing that Sean and I are on shaky ground. The only real thing we have in common is him. After talking to Shelby, I took a hot shower and climbed in my bed to take a nap. I was shocked to wake up the next morning at 8am. I must have been dog tired. I didn't even wake up to pee.

I reached over and grabbed my cell. I saw that mama had called to check on me. I called her back, and told her that I was okay, but had fallen asleep and was just waking up. She said her and daddy took turns staying with Andrew, and now Ashlynn was with him. She and daddy had gone home to get some rest.

I needed to let off some steam so I got dressed and headed to the gym. The boxing class I take there every so often was going to start in an hour. What better way to release stress and tension then punching shit. An hour later I was covered in sweat, my curls pulled up into a messy ponytail. I felt better, my mind more clear, my shoulders a lot lighter. I showered at the gym then headed back to Kaiser.

I walked into Andrew's room. He and Ashlynn were watching Maury. A day of healing had done him well. His face had gone down considerably. He was starting to look like my Chip again. I stood in the doorway and smiled at him. He and Ashlynn hadn't even noticed I was in the room, they were too engrossed in Ashlynn's favorite guilty pleasure show. Ashlynn turned and saw me standing there smiling.

"What's up Drea, how long you been standing there being a creeper?" She said.
"I just got here actually, y'all were so into the show I didn't want to interrupt." I said.

"SHE is into the show, you know I don't be watching this shit." Andrew said.

"You look much better today, how are you feeling though?" I asked him.

"I feel better. Still hurting of course, but I feel much better than yesterday. Having these fine ass nurses in here checking on me don't hurt either." He said, with a smirk.

"Yea, they feel sorry for you Drew. They don't know you're the male version of my fine ass under all that puffy ass skin and bruises." Ashlynn said winking at him.

We all laughed. It felt good that after all that had happened that my family was still just as strong as ever, they have always been all I needed. Suddenly, My mind drifted to Sean. His beautiful smile flashed into my daydream. I felt an ache growing inside of me, I missed him. I love him. I wish it was easy as flipping a switch, I would just turn the love off.

I stayed at the hospital with my brother and sister for a good 4 hours. Andrew said he had had enough company, and didn't need any more babysitting. He told us we could both go home. I made sure he was being serious before I gathered my things to head out. Ashlynn asked me to go grab something to eat with her. I heard my stomach answer her for me. I followed her to Chilis in Inglewood. We got seated and ordered drinks-- I knew I needed one-- the biggest they had! As our drinks arrived I looked up at Ashlynn, she didn't look like herself. Her big brown eyes were low, her head was down, ponytail hanging over her shoulder, her dimples flashed every time she chewed on her straw. Her beautiful caramel skin had even lost some of its glow. I was suddenly worried about her. With all that was going on in my personal life, Ash kind of had gotten lost in the shuffle.

"Ash, you okay?" I asked, concerned.

"Yea, I guess so." she said, still chewing on her straw.

"You don't look okay. You look, I don't know, kinda sad."

"I don't really want to talk about it Drea." She said, still not making eye contact.

"Ash, remember who you're talking to. I'm your big sister. I know when something is bothering you. I'll leave it alone if you want me to though. I won't ask. . ."

"Damn Drea, you sure know how to work a sista!" Ashlynn said shaking her head at me. "You know I can't keep anything from you."

"I know, so I don't even know why you try."

"Well. . . you know that guy Marcus that I had been talking to for the past few months?"

"Yea, the brown skin, tall cutie with them waves for days, and the dimples who came to take you to lunch a few times?"

"Damn Drea you really was checking him out huh?"

"Hey I can look! And cute is cute. It's not against the law. But, what about him?"

"Well I liked him a lot. I even let go of my entire roster because I thought he deserved a fair chance, and you know that's not something I would normally do. I usually keep at least 3 in rotation." she said smiling at herself.

"Yea, I know how y'all hoe's roll." I said laughing.

Ashlynn shot me a dirty look with one eyebrow raised."Whateva, not everyone wants their pussy to be deprived like you. That don't make me a hoe. I'm just. . . adventurous." She said sitting up straight, pursing her lips pretending to be classy. "Anyway, Me and Marcus were going strong, he had that bomb dick! You know what I mean! And I was sprung! So sprung that about a month ago we stopped using condoms."

Ashlynn's head was down. I knew exactly where this conversation was heading.

"Ash, are you pregnant?" I asked lifting her head so her eyes met mine.

"I don't know Drea, I could be. And I am so scared to tell Marcus. I know he likes me and all, but I don't know how he would feel about this info. I don't even know how I feel about it." She said, eyes watering.

"Damn Ash. . . I don't even know what to say. What are you gonna do? You're only 21, just a baby yourself."

"I know that, and I really have no clue. I'm so confused. I haven't even taken a pregnancy test yet. I don't want it to be real. Mama and daddy are gonna be so disappointed. Look at me, following right in Drew's footsteps." She said, lowering her head again.

"Well look, I won't pass judgement. I'll just be there for you, whatever you decide to do. Lets get some food in us, and then we'll go across the street to WalGreens and get a test." Ashlynn shook her head in agreement.

We grabbed a test and drove over to my place so that she could take it. That 30 seconds seemed like forever.

"Pregnant." Ashlynn said, walking out of the bathroom.

She collapsed on my bed next to me. Ashlynn cried like a baby for about 15 minutes as I rubbed her back. Her wild, impulsive lifestyle had caught up with her. She finally stopped crying, and looked up at me with pleading eyes. I knew she wanted me to have the answers, but this time, I just didn't.

CHAPTER ELEVEN

ANDREA

After finding out she was pregnant, Ashlynn decided to call Marcus and see how he felt about things. She didn't want to make any decisions without his input. He was, after all, the baby's father, and his opinion mattered too. Marcus wasn't too pleased with the pregnancy news. "I thought we were being careful." he told her. Ashlynn was so upset by his reaction she hung up on him. She had a lot of thinking to do. Ashlynn knew that whatever she decided to do would be all on her at that point. She informed Marcus, then me, a week after finding out that she was going to roll the dice and keep it. Ashlynn said she couldn't justify an abortion, and she didn't think she could go through with one anyway. Now she had to tell the family. We both knew it wouldn't go over well.

"How'd you let this happen!" Mama said looking at Ashlynn, then me.

Since Ashlynn was born, it was always my responsibility to look out for her "You're the big sister, it's your job" is what I always heard. I have tried her whole life to make sure she stays on the right track, but some things, like *this,* are just out of my hands. It wasn't my job to make sure she protected herself, so I don't know why mama was looking at me.

Ashlynn sat there leaning back on the couch, staring up at the ceiling. She knew our parents would be upset, so she asked me to be there to support her. For some reason I felt like I was in trouble too. Daddy sat across the room on the loveseat not saying a word.

"Well Phil, aren't you going to say something." Mama said, looking at daddy.

"I could say a lot of things. I could be really pissed. I could tell Ashlynn how big of a mistake she's made. I could hurt that boy who helped her get into this position, but really babe, what is that gonna do? She's pregnant now. She's decided to keep the child. We just have to deal with it. And don't get me wrong, I'm not happy about the situation, not even a little bit. The last thing I want is for my baby to be having a baby." Dad said.

Mama looked at him with a blank expression on her face. I know that's not the reaction she thought he would give. When Andrew came and told them that Kelly was pregnant, Daddy ripped him a new one. He told him how stupid he was, and how he would regret getting "a girl like that" pregnant. He didn't speak to Andrew for at least a month so I understood why mama looked so confused.

"Ashlynn, you know this hurts your daddy don't you?" Daddy said, looking Ashlynn in the eyes. "I wanted my kids to be in love and married before they started families. I really thought me and your mama had set a good example for you kids."

"Daddy, I'm not trying to hurt you or mama. Y'all know I didn't plan this shi. . I didn't plan this." Ashlynn said looking at them both. She let out a deep sigh and said,"I should have been more responsible with my body, and I know that, but I just couldn't even think about getting rid of it. It's just not in me, my heart wouldn't let me even go there."
I grabbed her hand and squeezed it. Ashlynn looked at me with a half smile.

"Baby, this is going to be really hard for you. I'm disappointed, but I know your daddy is right. All we can do it move forward." Mama said, pulling Ashlynn up into a hug.
Ashlynn cried in mama's arms, like all the pain she had ever felt was being released. Daddy came up behind her and hugged her too. Now we were all crying. I got up and joined in on the hugging. Telling our parents hadn't been as bad as we thought. We were going to be okay, and I was going to be an auntie again!

Sean

I hadn't heard from Andrea for about a week. When I wasn't at work, I spent a lot of time with mom, or over at Shelbys. I needed to be around people I knew loved me, and weren't going to judge me for my fuck up. I already felt bad enough. Mom was upset with me when I told her what had happened. She was upset with herself for giving Janae my number. She never expected anything like this to happen. I made sure she knew that none of this was her fault, it was all on me. Mom made sure I knew that she was here for me for whatever, just as a mother should be.

Shelby on the other hand ripped me a new one. She went on and on about how I could lose "The One" because I had a point to prove. She went on to tell me that if her husband Lamont ever done anything like that, she would probably consider walking out on him too. She told me that breaking a woman's trust is a huge no-no, and she knew that's how Andrea felt right now. While she cussed me out, I listened. I took in everything she said to me, because I knew she was right. She and Lamont had what I was trying to achieve, a healthy, loving marriage and family. I was too old to be playing any kind of games. It was time for me to grow up.

By the time Friday rolled around I drove over to Shelby's house to pick up Justin. I was taking him to my place for the weekend. Shelby deserved a much needed and very overdue break. She and Lamont had planned a romantic, kid-free weekend, and I was happy I could be there for them. Aside from that, I missed Justin. Some toddler fun was just what I needed.

I walked through Shelby's front door.

"Shel! How many times do I have to tell you, y'all aren't white! Stop leaving your front door unlocked." I scolded.

"Sean calm down with all that noise. I usually lock the doors." She said, hugging me.

"Well how come EVERYTIME I come over here, it's unlocked fool?" I said as I hugged her back.

"Whatever big head, just mind ya bidness." She said, slapping me on the shoulder.

I loved my cousin, my best friend, but she could be so hard headed.

"Oh, and thank you again for keeping Justin this weekend. Stella is trying to get her groove back!" She said, doing the butterfly to no music.

I stared at her shaking my head. Justin walked in the room and saw me, his face lit up.

"I guess my boy is happy to see me." I said, pointing to Justin. Anything to get Shelby to stop dancing.

"Yea I told him he was going to hang out with Uncle Sean this weekend, and he was pumped, isn't that right little man." She said, picking him.

I envied their relationship. I wanted to be a father someday. I wanted to raise a child from birth, and be there for him or her always. I could never see myself being an absentee parent. At that moment, I couldn't help but to think about Andrea. She was who I wanted to see my happily ever after with.

I grabbed Justin's things as Shelby put his carseat into my truck. She kissed him, and told him to be good. Shelby and I hugged.

"Have a good weekend Stella." I told her, as I hopped into my driver's seat.

"Oh I will!" She said, in the driveway doing the butterfly again.

"You're a damn nut! I'll call you if I need anything." I said backing out.

"I hope you don't need anything, and I'll try not to stalk my baby while he's with you." She said, still dancing.

I tossed up a peace sign and drove back to the City of Champions. Me and Justin had a full evening of playing, and cartoon watching. I was ready to get to it, and try and take my mind off of Andrea. I was still trying to give her the space she asked for. I just hoped it wasn't permanent.

Justin had been great all weekend. On Sunday before I took him home, something compelled me drive over to Torrance and visit Robbins Bros. an engagement ring store. I wasn't sure what I was gonna get, but I was going to leave with something.

Justin helped me pick out the perfect gifts. I got something beautiful for all of the important women in my life. I stopped by Mom's first. She hadn't seen her nephew in a while, and asked me to bring him by.

"Look how big he is now!" Mom said as she let us in.

"I know, I can't believe he'll be 2 soon, they grow up so fast."

"Who you tellin'." Mom said, taking Justin from my arms.

"I got you something."I said, pulling the blue box out of the bag.

"Sean, baby, what did you do." She said, smiling, opening the box. Inside was a sparkling diamond necklace in the shape two hearts intertwined.

Mom looked at me misty eyes. She sat Justin down on the floor, and hugged me.

"What did I do to deserve such a beautiful piece of jewelry?" She said, taking it out of the box and holding it up into the sun beaming through her living room window.

"You didn't have to DO anything Mom. You are a wonderful mother, a great woman, and an all around awesome person. I just wanted you to have something you could keep as a token of my appreciation." I said, taking the necklace from her hands and putting it on her neck.

She couldn't stop her tears from flowing as she hugged me. I was glad I could make her happy. She's always done her best to do that for me.

I got Justin, and headed to Shelby's place. When I got there she was outside watering the grass. Justin was happy to see her. Lamont walked out front and scooped his son up. We dapped and he went over and kissed Shelby. Judging by their body language, they had a good weekend.

"How you been Bro?" I asked Lamont. He works so much, I hardly ever see him.

Lamont was a big guy. Shelby called him her big chocolate teddy bear. He was 6'5' inches 265 lbs and solid muscle. Shelby always looked like a little girl standing next to him. All 5'3" of her had nothing on her massive husband. If you didn't know him, you'd think he was a mean dude, but he is one of the nicest guys I knew.

"I been good man, just working my tail off. Business has been really good."

"That's what up! I'm glad it's working out."

"Yea man, It was touch and go for awhile. I even had to hire a few more guys. As long as people need things remodeled I'll stay in business." He said with a laugh.

"I'm sure they will, especially out here in the land of unlocked doors." I said, both of us looking at Shelby.

"I'll start locking the damn doors! Sheesh!" She said, smiling and shaking her head at us.

"Oh, before I forget, me and Justin got you a gift Shel," I told her, reaching into the bag. I handed the box to Justin, and told him to give it to his mommy. Shelby opened the box smiling at us. Inside was a beautiful pair of diamond heart shaped earrings that sparkled as the sun kissed them.

"Sean! Justin! These are beautiful!" She said, hugging me around the neck, then kissing Justin.

"Justin picked them out. He has really good taste." I said.

"Those are dope! You trying to make me look bad." Lamont said, with a smile.

"Naw, nothing like that." I said laughing." Shelby is just my best friend, my cousin, my. . . she's just awesome."

"Sean, I know I'm the greatest, you didn't have to do this." She said, staring at the earrings."

"I know I didn't have to, I wanted to. I just wanted something to show you how much I appreciate you. You're always there for me, and I love you like no other." I told her.

"Aww cuzzo! You're trying to knock the thug right out of me!" Shelby said, wiping a tear from her eye. It was very rare for her to cry, so I know I had done good.

"Well I'm gonna head out of there. I have some things to do. Y'all enjoy the rest of your Sunday." I said, as I got in my truck.

Shelby, Lamont and Justin stood there waving at me as I drove away. They looked like the perfect little family.

CHAPTER TWELVE

ANDREA

I haven't had any contact with Sean in about two weeks, I was too upset, and probably overreacting, but I felt like I was right for feeling the way I did. Before all of this happened, we would talk on the phone a few times a day, and see each other at least every other. I was realizing more each day just how much I missed him, and how much he had become part of my routine. To try and fill up some space in my life when I wasn't working, I spent time trying to catch up with Jamie. She wasn't too happy that it seemed like I had abandoned her for a man. I hadn't realized it, but I guess she was right. Jamie was my best friend, and I hadn't spent time with her in months, and we rarely talked on the phone any more. Sean and I had spent more time with each other than with anyone else. I've always been the girl to tell my friends not to change up for a man, and yet I've done it myself.

I asked Jamie to meet me for brunch at the Proud Bird. She showed up right on time, wearing a blue flower print maxi dress. She looked lovely as usual, and I even think I saw a hint of a smile she was trying to hide as she walked in. I felt nervous, I knew she was going to lay into me for falling off. I had stood her up a few times to go and do things with Sean instead. Jamie had stopped calling me as much because she said I hadn't had much time for her. Friendship is a two way street, and I had turned it into feeling more like a one lane highway with all my flakiness. I had to just take whatever she was going to dish out, because I knew I deserved it. I also needed her to get it out of her system so I could tell her what was going on between me and Sean.

"Long time no see stranger." She said, as she walked toward me.

"I know J. I'm sorry." I said, reaching my arms out to hug her.

Jamie resisted for a second, then she broke down, smiled, and hugged me. One thing she and I could never do, was stay mad at each other long.

"I've missed you Pooh." She said hugging me tighter.

"I've missed you too babes. Now stop hugging me before you make me cry." I told her.

We giggled like schoolgirls then asked to be seated at the bar.

We caught up over Mimosas and seafood omelets. She told me that everything for her had been great. Her husband Lance had got a promotion, and was now a full time banker at Chase. Her dance studio had taken on more students, so business was great. The girls were getting big, Bella's 4th birthday was in 2 weeks.

I was happy things were going so great for her. I promised I would never fall off again. I had to fill her in about all the things that had been happening to me within the last 2 weeks. I told her about what Kelly had done to Andrew. She was only upset for a hot second that I hadn't called her. I didn't want to worry anyone else with that. We were all already stressed out, so she understood. I told her about Ashlynn's pregnancy. Jamie was shocked. "I can't imagine that little heffa being anyone's mama." She said. I agreed, but told her we all needed to be there for her. That kid didn't know what it was in for with Ashlynn as a mother.

I sucked in as much air as I could, and let it out slowly, I had to tell her about Sean. I told her everything that had gone down, and how I was feeling about it now. I even told her about Mark showing up at my house that day. She was so annoyed with Mark, she cringed when she heard his name. Jamie was always the level headed voice of reason so I knew she would lead me in the right direction.

"Damn Drea, that's a lot." she said, rubbing my shoulder.

"I know, and I really don't know what to do about it."

"I see why you're upset Pooh, I would be too." She said.

"What do you think I should do? Should I end it officially? I haven't talked to him in 2 weeks."

"I can't tell you to do that. What I can tell you though is that I liked Sean. The few times I've been around him, what I could tell is that he was all about you. I know he loves you."

"I lo. . ." I paused and got quiet.

"You what Drea? You love him too? It's okay to say it. I know that fuck head Mark broke you down, but Sean and Mark are completely different."

"I know, but I just knew adding love in the mix would make things really real. I was scared to go there. We've been dating for almost 9 months, and I have never uttered those words to him." I confessed.

"Has he said them to you?" She asked.

"I think so... I don't know. If he has, I've blocked it out because I wasn't ready to receive that yet." I said, putting my head down.

"Maybe you should tell him how you really feel. I know he fucked up, but it's not something that's unforgivable in my eyes, and you know I'd tell you if that's how I felt." she said.

"I know, that's why I wanted to hear it from you. The only other person who knows anything about this is Ashlynn, and that's because she saw him. You know how irrational she can be."

"Yea, I know. She can be a bit off the wall. And I can't believe that turd showed up at your house!" She hated saying Mark's name, so she never did.

"Ugh, don't even mention Mark, I could have killed him."

We sat and talked for two hours before we headed out. I promised Jamie I would talk to Sean and we promised things would go back to normal between us. We needed each other; we always have.

Sean

Today had been a great day. I made two very important women in my life very happy, and I was thinking about breaking my own record, and possibly going for three. Driving up LaBrea, I stopped at the light on Centinela right near Andrea's boutique. I was in a zone listening to the new John Legend album when I heard a car honk. A familiar voice yelled my name. I turned to my right and saw Eli flagging me down. We pulled into the Pizza Hut parking lot across the street. Eli hopped out of his Camaro and I hopped out of my SUV. We double slapped hands and Eli said, "Damn dude you went from no bitches, to being practically married, and now I hardly see you anymore Bro, where they do that at?"

"It's not even like that dude, you know you my ace!"

"Yea, yea whateva Bro. Every time I call you to hang out, you already got plans with Andrea. I haven't even seen your punk ass in at least two month." He said, slapping me in the back of the head.

Eli was right, my world has become all about me and Andrea. That's just how it is when you actually enjoy the person you're spending time with, and I loved spending time with Andrea. Sitting here talking to Eli, I realized how much I missed hanging with my boy too. I just wasn't down for the chasing women part like he was. The thrill in that had passed and I was only interested in one woman.

"Me and Andrea have hit a snag right now anyway." I told him, looking down at my feet.

"What you mean a snag? Who fucked up, you or her? Spill it."

"Well It was me." I confessed.

I went on to tell him the entire story about Janae, and how the whole thing went down with Andrea. He leaned on his car with his arms crossed in front of his chest, shaking his head. The next thing out of his mouth was unexpected.

"Bro, you were trippin! Why would you even give a bitch, who used to give you no play, any time of day. Now her ass is lonely, and she comes looking for you? You shoulda told that broad to swerve, and kept it moving'." He said, looking at me very intently.

"Wow Eli." I said, my mouth hanging open, "I was sure you were gonna tell me Andrea was trippin', and needed to get it together." I confessed.

"Normally that's what I would say, but I've been around Andrea, she really is a good girl and BAD with some extra D's like you said. I don't even think I would fuck that one up. So now what you gon do Bro?"

"I was actually on my way over to her place right now."

"Maybe you should call first. I don't think you should pop up on her if she told you she needed space." He suggested.

"Well my pops told me actions speak much louder than words, I want to go over there and show her how I feel." I said, reaching in my truck to show him the gift I got her.

"Aw Bro, that's nice as hell. If she doesn't take you back after seeing that grand gesture, it might really be over."

I didn't want to hear that, but he was right. If I lay all my cards out there, and she still rejects me, things are beyond repair.

I thanked my boy for his advice, double slapped hands with him and we both hopped back in our rides and went on with our day.

I decided to take Eli's advice and call Andrea before just popping up. Her cell rang a few times, then went to voicemail. I decide to leave a message.

"Uhh. . . hey Andrea, this is Sean. I know you said you needed space, but I would really like to see you. I have some things to say to you, and I also have something I want to give you. Please give a call when you're free. Uhh. . . I. . . I guess that's it. Hope to talk to you soon."

Andrea

After brunch with Jamie, I headed over to Kaiser. Andrew was being released from the hospital today. Tylor had been staying with my parents since his mom had been arrested. Before the police even had the cuffs tightly around Kelly's wrists, my parents had been down to the courthouse to file a motion on behalf of Andrew to get an emergency custody order for Ty. Andrew was half past ready to get back to his normal life. Kelly was being held on a number of charges including assault for arranging my brother's beating. She was definitely going to serve some time for what she had done.

After Andrew was released, he decided to stay with my parents for a little while. He figured he could continue to recuperate there while his bones healed, and my parents could continue to help him with Tylor. It all sounded like a great plan to me. After making sure Andrew was safely home with my parents, I headed home. I pulled out my cell to see I had a missed call and message from Sean. Seeing his name on my phone made my heart flutter. I pressed the voicemail button and listened to his message. He asked for me to call him, because he wanted to talk, and had something for me. I was conflicted. I wasn't sure I was ready to see him yet, I still needed to sort out my feelings. I figured I could tell him that in person, I shot him a quick text.

"I'm headed home, meet me there."

I pulled up to my place to find Sean already parked out front. Suddenly I was very nervous. I didn't know what I was going to say to him and I had no clue what the end result of whatever was going to go down would be. What I knew for sure was that a conversation needed to be had and cards needed to be laid on the table.

Sean took a minute to get out of his truck. I walked into the house, leaving the door open for him. I picked Sugar up and sat on the couch waiting for him. He walked in a moment later, closing the door behind him. He looked better than usual. His hair was freshly cut and he was wearing a royal blue polo shirt, and dark blue jeans. Blue was definitely his color. I tried to hide how excited I was to see him, but Sugar didn't. She jumped off my lap and ran right over to him.

She jumped up on him until he picked her up and rubbed her behind her ears, just the way she liked. He put her down and came over to the couch sitting down next to me. I could tell he was trying to read how I was feeling. He wasn't sure if he should touch me, and since he walked in, I hadn't said a word, or made much eye contact. I really wanted him to say what he had to say, before I got started with what I needed to get off my chest. We sat there in silence for a few moments. I wanted so badly to hug and kiss him, and lay my head on his shoulder like I had gotten so used to doing. We both began to speak at the same time.

"So listen." We both said in unison.

We laughed a little. That broke the awkwardness a little bit.

"You first." I told him, giving him the floor.

Sean

I sat across from Andrea trying to gather my words. I couldn't read her today. Usually she was so transparent, but today, I just didn't know. I wanted Andrea to know I was sincere, so I decided just to speak from my heart and throw all the pretense out the window.

"Andrea, I am so sorry. I never meant to hurt you in any way. All I have wanted since the day we met was to make you happy, especially since that's all you've ever done for me. You are always the first person on my mind when I wake up and the last on my mind when I go to sleep. I love everything about you from your curly hair to those 26 freckles on your face. I love how you have the ability to make everyone around you fall in love with you without even trying. I knew I wanted to be with you since before you knew I existed. I know God answers prayers, because he brought you into my life. You are my whole world Andrea LaSalle. You are my everything, and I can't go another day without you in my life. I love you baby. I love you so much it hurts. I'm here, right now to SHOW you that I mean it. My words mean nothing without my actions."

Andrea sat across from me with tears in her eyes as I poured my heart out to her. I stopped for a moment to let her speak.

"I have more to say, but if you need to tell me anything before I go on, please do." I told her.

Andrea buried her face into the couch cushions. I could hear her low sobs. I got close to her, and wrapped my arms around her.

"Andrea, baby, I'm sorry. I'm so sorry. I'll leave if you want me to." I said between tears.

"No. Don't leave. These aren't sad tears. I've been holding something in for awhile now too. I need to get something off my chest." She said.

Andrea

I couldn't believe I lost it like that. All those wonderful things Sean was saying, and all I could do was sob. I wasn't expecting him to be so intense. He looked me straight into my eyes with every word his spoke. I could feel his passion. All of my emotions were starting to bubble over. I needed to tell Sean the truth about how I was feeling.

"Sean, you know I've been hurt before. I never wanted to experience that type of pain again. When I love, I love hard, and I can't half ass that. I love you Sean. I've loved you for awhile now, probably since our first date. I couldn't bring myself to tell you that, because I NEEDED you to tell me first. I didn't want to be in a relationship where the person I loved didn't love me back. I also didn't want you to tell me you loved me, because you thought that was what I wanted to hear. So, I never said it, although I wanted to plenty of times. Sean, baby, you make me feel like the most beautiful girl in the world. When I'm with you, the earth stands still. You have made me believe in love again and for that, I am truly grateful." I confessed though my tears. I was ugly crying, but at the moment I didn't even care. I needed him to feel everything I was feeling. I needed him to know that I loved him. I needed him to know that I didn't want to live without him.

"I need you to know that I need you in my life, no matter the capacity. If you just want to be friends, I'll take it. I just can't lose you." Sean said, his hands cupping both sides of my face.He placed the softest kiss on my lips. I felt like our souls were intertwined at that moment. I loved him. I couldn't fight it any longer. I wrapped my arms around his neck and kissed him with all the passion I had inside of me. Tears falling from both of our eyes as our tongues made themselves familiar again. We had missed each other; it was apparent.

Sean stopped kissing me to look me in my eyes. I nodded slowly, giving him permission to proceed. He stood me up in front of him not saying a word. He turned me around, and unzipped my sundress slowly. Kissing the back of my neck, he unfastened my strapless bra. He undressed me in silence. He stood back, and admired me like he was seeing me for the first time. We smiled at each other as he took off his shirt. I moved close to him, unbuckled his belt, unbuttoned his jeans and his pants fell down to his shoe. Sean smiled at me; his erection was poking through his briefs. He stepped out of his shoes and pants, and moved over to me. He pulled me into him, kissing me passionately. Something about that kiss made my insides quiver. I let out a soft moan as he kissed down my chest, paying close attention to to my breasts. He feasted on them with such desire, I felt the wetness building between my legs. Sean made his way back up to my lips, and kissed them gently. He walked to the sofa, and grabbed my soft fleece throw blanket; spreading it out on the floor. He tossed a few pillows down onto the blanket. He grabbed my hand and lead me over to the love nest he had made. I followed his lead.

Sean

I laid Andrea down on the love nest I had just created for us. After our confessions, we hadn't spoken a word. She had allowed me to kiss her, and I was thrilled. I was sure she was done with me. Now I have her undressed and I'm ready to show her how much I love her. I slid Andrea out of her panties; she raised her hips to assist me. I took my briefs off and positioned myself between her legs. I grabbed both of her thighs and pulled her toward me. I was about to devour her, and show her how much I had missed her. Andrea tasted better; sweeter than I before. Her moans were like sweetest love song. I heard her hit notes I hadn't heard before. Andrea came quicker than she ever had with me. Everything about this experience was different than before. She laid there panting for a few seconds. She grabbed my arms, and pulled me on top of her. I hovered there, touching the warmth and wetness between her legs. Andrea looked me deep into my eyes and slid a hand down my side, to her thigh, and over my manhood. She stroked me a few times, never taking her eyes off of mine. She opened her thighs wide and slid me inside of her. She was hot, wet and tight. I couldn't believe what was happening, but I went with it. She moved her hips back and forth as I hovered there, not sure if I should participate. She pulled me down; letting me know it was okay. I relaxed on top of her, lifting one of her thighs. I slid myself deeper inside of her and we both let out a simultaneous moan. Right there, on the floor of her living room Andrea and I made love.

Andrea

I awoke this morning wrapped in a throw blanket on the floor. The aroma of scrambled cheese eggs, pancakes and bacon floated from my kitchen. A smile crept across my face with thoughts of the night before. I confessed my love for Sean, and things happened afterwards that I would never have imagined. He and I had grown closer in the last few hours than we had in the nine months we had known each other. I never knew that being openly in love with someone would feel like this.

Sean came back into the living room, naked, with a tray of food in front of him. I smiled at him, shaking my head.

"Good morning baby." He said, sitting down next to me on the floor, " I made you breakfast."

"Thank you, I woke up starving." I said, kissing his cheek.

Sean looked at me with this grin on his face, like he wanted to say something.

"What's that look about?" I asked, taking a bite of my bacon.

I followed his eyes down to my plate. On the tip of my fork was a solitaire, princess cut diamond ring. I looked back over at Sean who was on one knee.

"Andrea, remember last night, when I told you I had something for you? This ring," He said, removing it from the fork, and holding it up in front of me as his hands trembled "is for you. I want you to know that you mean everything to me. I can't imagine going through the rest of this life without you. Will you be my wife?" He asked, pure joy written all over his face.

I didn't know what to say. We had just told each other we love one another for the first time last night. Marriage seemed a little sudden, not that it hadn't crossed my mind. There was one thing I knew for sure, I didn't want to spend the rest of my life without him either.

"Yes!" I said, with a wide smile "Yes I'll marry you!"

He slid the ring on my finger; it fit like it was made just for me.

"You don't know how happy you just made me baby!" He said, kissing me.

"You know, even though I already said yes, you still have to ask my dad." I said smiling, only half joking.

"Can we go over there today? I want to do it however you'd like. I'll even ask Ashlynn if I have to." He said wrapping his arms around me.

"Hey, what's in that other box?" I asked, referring to a second small blue box that was next to his jeans.

"Oh," he said grabbing it,"This was for you too, just in case things hadn't ended up this way."

I took the box from him and opened it. There was a necklace inside with a diamond charm dangling from it in the shape of a star.

"This is pretty too, but it's no engagement ring." I said, smiling at him.

"I didn't know if I'd leave here without you being my lady, but I wanted you to have something from me. You are the moon and the stars to me babe. Even if we weren't together I wanted you to always remember that."

Sean was leaned back on his elbows. I put the tray down and climbed on top of him. Without a word I kissed him. I knew right then that forgiving Sean was the best choice I could have made. He was my love, my one of a kind love, and I would never let him go, not again.

We made love again, on the same love nest from the night before. Only this time, I was his wife to be.

Epilogue

Sean

I can't believe this day has finally come. It's been 14 months of frustration, planning and preparation, but today is our wedding day. Andrea was certain she wanted a spring wedding, and it was my job to make sure got everything she wanted. I could hardly wait for her to become Mrs. Williams. Andrea was one of a kind, and I couldn't wait to spend the rest of my forevers with her.

"Aye Bro, you almost ready?" Eli said, stepping into the men's dressing room at the banquet hall.

"I'm beyond ready." I said, smiling at him.

Eli looked dapper in his dark blue suit with teal, purple and navy paisley print tie. He had cut his braids off, and was now sporting tapered curls. He looked so different; more mature. Over the last year my friend had indeed grown up. Eli had finally met a woman he felt was worth his time. He had planned to do right by her, and so far he had done so.

"You look good bro," he said, adjusting my tie,"almost as good as me."

We shared a laugh. So much had changed but our friendship was stronger than ever.

There was a knock at the door, we both turned in its direction. Andrew and Tylor walked in, both matching Eli exactly. My groomsmen were fly--if I do say so myself.

"Uncle Sean, you like my suit?" Ty asked, spinning around.

"Yea man, you look sharp." I told him, slapping him a high five."You too Drew! Man we all look dope today. Drea knew what she was doing picking this color scheme"

"Me too!" Justin said, bursting through the door followed by my dad.

My dad moved to Cali a month after I proposed to Andrea. When we decide who we wanted to be in our wedding party, my dad was a no brainer. Little did he know, he was the one who pushed me to propose to Andrea. He and I had formed a bond that was so strong that I had forgiven him for not being there during my childhood.

All of my guys looked great. If we were any indication of what the ladies looked like, we would definitely take the crown for best looking wedding party. Today was going to be an unforgettable day, I couldn't wait to see my bride.

Andrea

"I'm so nervous, my guts are bubbling." I said out loud.

"Girl you better go poop before we get you into your dress." Jamie said.

"Yea, with your nasty ass." Ashlynn said, holding her daughter Bree who had just turned 5 months. "Auntie is a nasty little stinker ain't she boo boo."Bree laughed.
Shelby sat off to the side laughing." I know the feeling girl, I felt the same way before my wedding." She said, rubbing her growing belly. She and her husband Lamont are expecting a baby girl in the summer. She was glowing.
All my girls looked beautiful in their dresses. Each of them got to pick which length they liked best. I knew I had to pick something that all of them could wear again. We ended up agreeing on a dress that was navy lace on top with a satin purple underlay. Shelby had to get hers let out for the wedding. Her and Lamont hadn't been trying to have another baby, but they weren't not trying to have a baby either.

"You guys, promise I don't look like a whale in this dress." Shelby asked, turning to the side.

"Girl please, you look damn good. All you gained was a belly. When I was pregnant with my girls people thought I was just getting fat, because that's what happened before I got the belly. You don't have that issue." Jamie said, laughing, rubbing Shelby's belly.

Shelby had become one of my closest friends. She hung out with Jamie and I often.

"Jamie hush it, your body is bangin! I wish I had legs like yours." Ashlynn said, bouncing Bree on her lap.

"Yea these are some nice gams if I do say so myself," Jamie said, strutting across the room in her teal peep toes." And my hubby loves them too. It's a wonder I'm not in the pregnant club right now too." We all laughed. Jamie and I shared a smile.

Jamie and her husband Lance still acted like newlyweds after all of these years. It was so sickeningly sweet. Her girls, my flower girls, were both getting so big and pretty. They were in the mirror showing off their ballet moves in their pretty teal dresses. Jamie had been teaching the girls to dance since before they could walk. Her dance studio was doing so well she had to hire more instructors to teach the influx of kids they were getting.

"Look at my girls; they can really move." Jamie said, smiling fondly at her babies.

After I got the finishing touches on my make up, I was ready to get into my dress. It was a beautiful white lace mermaid style gown with a sweetheart neckline. It showed all of the curves my Sean loved so much.

"Baby, you look absolutely beautiful!" Mama said as she came into the dressing room, her eyes welling up with tears.

"Aww thank you mama. You look beautiful too! Don't cry, you're gonna mess up your makeup." I told her. Mama had on a navy blue ball gown. She said she was not going to be seen in anyone's "Mother of The Bride" frumpiness. She was definitely killing them in her gown.

"Thank you baby," she said, striking a pose." Your daddy could barely keep his hands off of me."

"Mama, come on now, we don't need to hear or visualize that. I'm not trying to lose my breakfast." Ashlynn teased.

"Okay baby, I know you're not trying to play innocent." Mama said, pointing to Bree. We all shared a laugh. It was nice that I could keep my mind off my nerves. I knew once I saw Sean I would be a complete mess.

Ashlynn got a text, grinned, and said she would be back. She passed Bree to Mama and was out the door.

"Damn baby, you look so good! I couldn't wait any longer to see you."

"You look damn good too. That suit is yummy on you." Ashlynn said, biting her bottom lip.

"Don't bite your lip, you know what that does to me."

"I know, and you know what YOU do to me." She said, stepping close to her guy.

While Ashlynn was pregnant she and Marcus tried to make things work for the sake of their child. He told her before she was too far along, that he thought it would be a better idea if she terminated her pregnancy. Ashlynn stood her ground, and told Marcus that he didn't have to stick around if he didn't want to. She was prepared to raise her child on her own. After months of fussing and fighting, Ashlynn broke up with Marcus. They agreed that he would be there for the baby when she came, but they weren't going to keep pretending like things were working between them.

Ashlynn delivered a healthy 7lb 8oz baby girl with all of us there. Marcus chose not to be in the room so he stayed in the waiting area. Six weeks later, Ashlynn's body had snapped back into pre-baby condition, right in time for our first meeting with our wedding party. Our wedding would be in 5 months, and we needed to get everything squared away. Sean and Eli were already in my living room when Ashlynn showed up. As soon as she walked in, Eli's chin hit the floor.

"Bro, who is that?" Eli asked Sean.

"That's Ashlynn, Andrea's little sister." Sean told him.

"She's beautiful." Eli said, not taking his eyes off of her.

That entire night, Eli was fairly quiet; nothing like his normal talkative, flirtatious self. I had never seen Eli like this. Sean told me later, he thought Eli had a thing for Ashlynn.

A week or so later Eli called me to ask me about her. I told him he could try his luck, but Ashlynn was mean when it came to men.

"If you don't want your feelings hurt, I wouldn't even bother." I advised

"I'll take my chances." was Eli's confident response.

The next time we all met up, Eli made his move. He sat next to Ashlynn and talked to her. For the first time in a while she was smiling. I couldn't believe she was falling for Eli's mack lines. Ashlynn told me later that he was sexy and sweet. They exchanged numbers, and continued to talk. After about a month, Ashlynn introduced Eli to Bree, and he was in love. Come to find out, Eli always wanted a family of his own. He told Sean that he never felt as strongly for a woman as he did for Ashlynn. Sean and I both noticed the change in him and Ashlynn. Eli wasn't about the chase anymore. He had let go of all his other girls, and focused solely on Ash and the baby. Ashlynn was happy. She gushed about Eli every chance she got. They were an odd pairing, but they seemed to fit together like puzzle pieces.

That was 4 months ago and they were still going strong.

"Where's my baby?" Eli asked her, kissing her on the lips.

"She's in the room with the girls.

"She's probably missing me, I should go get her."

"Eli if you don't leave her alone. She's fine in there, you'll get to see her in a little bit." Ashlynn said, shaking her head, laughing.

"Alright, I'm gonna let you get back in there before I have you out of that dress and on my lap." he said, sliding his hands down her back, cupping her butt.

"Don't start none, won't be none." Ashlynn said, kissing him softly before she walked away.

Eli stood in the hallway watching her.

"Dude if you don't get your ass back in here; don't make me knock you out looking at my sister like that." Andrew said, laughing.

"That's my baby right there." Eli said.

"Yea, and you treat her right too, so I won't rough you up." Andrew said, putting his arm around Eli's neck as the made their way back to the men's dressing room.

Andrew had been through a lot. About a month after his attack, the DA called and told him that they had built a case against Kelly, and his testimony would be necessary. He was more than willing to do what he needed to do to have her put away. Kelly was sentenced to 5 years with the possibility of parole after 30 months. She'd have a lot of time to herself. Hopefully she would think about how her actions lead her to where she was.

It took him much longer than he expected to heal from his injuries. He stayed with our parents until he felt like he was well enough to do things on his own. After about 5 months, he was able to get back to work and start living his life again. Things have been looking up for him. He's been the best daddy to Tylor. He told me that being a single father was the most fulfilling job, and the smile he and Tylor always had showed us all that they would be just fine. Andrew wasn't looking for a relationship, but he stumbled upon one recently when he met a sweet girl named Janae. Andrew was smitten with her. He brought her to a family dinner and it turned out she is the same Janae that I was mad at Sean about. We all talked and moved past that silliness. Janae is a cool girl. She told me and Sean that after that night they had in the parking lot, she was pissed for awhile. I told her how pissed I was at him too. She had figured out that she wasn't really in love with him, she just knew she deserved more than what she was settling for. Sean was the best example of how she wanted to be treated. When she met Andrew, neither of them were looking for anything, but things progressed naturally between them. They've been dating for 7 months and Ty loves her just as much as Andrew seems to.

It was almost time for our wedding to begin, and I was again a bundle of nerves. There was no turning back now. In 10 minutes I would be Mrs. Williams. It has such a nice ring to it.

Sean

"Where'd you go?" I asked Eli.

"He was out in the hall making eyes at my baby sister." Andrew said.

Eli didn't say a word, he just stood there smiling.

"That's the face of a man in love." my dad said.

"Mike be knowing what he's talking about." Eli said, giving a pound to my dad.

My dad did know what he was talking about. He and mom had gotten quite cozy since he moved back. They had taken the time to get to know each other and fall in love all over again. I had never seen my mom happier and it was really nice to have parents, with an s. I know that sounds strange, but having parents was new to me. With my blessing, my parents were married 6 months ago at the justice of the peace. Michael has treated my mom like the queen she is, and I couldn't be happier for them.

My mom walked me down the aisle. I kissed her on the cheek before helping her to her seat, pride written all over her face. I stood at the altar. The music started. *So Beautiful* by Musiq was playing.

"You're my baby,

My lover, my lady

All night

You make me

```
Want you
It drives me crazy
I feel like you were made just for me baby
Tell me if you feel the same way"
```

I told Andrea that song always made me think of her, and when I envisioned her walked down the aisle that was the song that played in my head. Today it would be a reality. Tylor and Justin walked down together and stood in front of me. Eli and Ashlynn walked down next, holding hands, making eyes at each other. You would have thought it was their wedding, they looked so natural together. Andrew walked down next with Jamie, followed by my dad and Shelby. She looked so beautiful all made up and pregnant. I could just imagine Andrea pregnant and glowing. One day that would be our reality too.

Giselle and Bella started down the aisle, tossing purple roses from their little baskets. Everything was happening just the way we planned. The double doors opened and everyone stood up.

Andrea

Once the doors opened, my nerves seemed to fade. Daddy kissed me on the cheek, and smiled at me. He looked so handsome in his navy suit, his salt and pepper curls silky and neat. Mama held my left arm as we walked toward my future. Sean and I couldn't take our eyes off of each other, as I approached the altar. His eyes started to water, as did mine as I took my final steps.

"Who gives this woman to be married to this man?" The minister asked.

"We do!" my parents said, in unison.

They both kissed me. Mama and Daddy both hugged Sean. Daddy whispered something in Sean's ear and went and took his seat. Sean took my hand and faced me. The minister was speaking, but I didn't hear a word he was saying. All I could concentrate on was how handsome Sean looked. I couldn't wait to kiss him for the first time as his wife.

"The bride and groom have written their own vows." I heard the minister say.

"Well we didn't write anything down, " Sean said.

"We're just going to speak from our hearts." I chimed in, looking Sean in the eyes.

"Well the bride and groom are going to speak from the heart." The minister said, smiling at us.

He handed Sean the microphone.

"Andrea Angelica LaSalle, soon to be William. I have been in love with you since the first time I laid eyes on you. I knew you were one of a kind from the moment we spoke. You have been nothing but true and faithful to me since we met, and I vow to be faithful and true to you for the rest of our lives. You are my best friend, my partner in crime, and the love of my life. I thank God every day for placing us together. I thank God everyday for you."

"That was beautiful Sean. You think you can top that Andrea?" The minister said, passing me the mic.

I took the mic with a smile." that was beautiful babe." I said, before clearing my throat.

"Sean Michael Williams, I had no plans on meeting you. I had completely given up on love. You came into my life at a time I think I needed you most. My faith in relationships had been crushed, and I was becoming disillusioned with the whole idea. The day we met I knew something was different. I knew I needed to give love one more shot. You are my one and only, my one of a kind love, and I will be forever grateful to God for placing us together. I vow to be true and faithful to you for the rest of our lives together. You are the ying to my yang, the Barack to my Michelle, the love of my life, and I can't wait to spend the rest of my life as your wife."

"Okay, she can hold her own." The minister said, taking back the mic.

We held hands, and repeated after the minister as he went through our traditional vows.

"It is now an honor that I pronounce you Husband and Wife, Mr. Williams, you may now kiss the new Mrs. Williams."

Sean lifted my veil slowly. He looked me deep in the eyes, then smiled. Sean placed a slow soft kiss on my lips. Everyone in the venue cheered. We had finally done it. We were husband and wife.

Sean

We were married! I could hardly believe it. I had a wife! I was someone's husband!

We walked outside and took pictures with our wedding party. I was smiling so hard my face was starting to hurt, but I didn't care. This was the best day of my life. Andrea looked more beautiful than I have ever seen her look. She was absolutely glowing.

After our guests had their cocktails, we were announced back into the reception. All of the groomsmen and the bridesmaids were introduced, dancing to Beyonce's *Single Ladies*. Then it was our turn to make our debut as husband and wife.

"Introducing Mr. and Mrs. Williams." The DJ announced.

We came through the doors dancing, Andrea waving her bouquet in the air. Then we took the floor for our first dance. I let Andrea pick the song, I had no idea what we would dance to.

Andrea

My Last First Kiss by Tamia came through the speakers. This song always made me think of Sean, so I knew I wanted to dance to it with him once I became his wife.

```
"When it comes to you I wouldn't change a thing
I wouldn't even change the things I could change
```

'Cause baby you're perfect, perfect to me
Simply means that you are perfect for me
You're the answer to a prayer I haven't prayed
Got me ready to settle down, I think I wanna say
I'm fallin' in love with you, I'm feeling all of this
Baby, I'm praying that you are
My last first kiss"

"This is a beautiful song baby." Sean said, holding me around the waist.

"I think of you, of us every time I hear it." I said, kissing him softly.

"I'm so happy you're my wife. I love you so much."

"I'm happy too, more happy than I have ever been."

"Me too, I can't wait until we start our family."

"You won't have to wait too long."

"Oh I know, we're gonna practice right after this." Sean said, kissing my neck.

"No need to practice daddy." I said, looking him straight in his eyes, still slow dancing.

"You mean. . ." Sean looked down at my stomach.

I smiled, holding him tight. "Yes, We're gonna have a baby."

"Dreams really do come true." Sean said, kissing me.

"And God made a believer out of me. I'm getting my happy ending, and you babe, are one of a kind."

Made in the USA
Columbia, SC
14 September 2021